WHO LET THE WOLVES OUT?

Peculiar Mysteries Book 9

RENEE GEORGE

Barkside of the Moon Press

Who Let The Wolves Out?

Peculiar Mysteries Book 9

Copyright © 2019 by Renee George

Publisher: Barkside of the Moon Press

Print ISBN: 978-1-947177-29-1

For my sister Robbin Clubb.
You have my back day and night 24/7. I would be a hot mess
without you!! I love your f*cking guts!
And for Robyn Peterman
(aka my Robyn Smith in the book),
Who called me twice a day to cheer me on,
I love your f*cking guts!

ACKNOWLEDGMENTS

For the usual suspects, BFF sister Robbin Clubb, who was with me every step of the way, BFF and favorite cookie Robyn Peterman, who called me twice a day to cheer me on, BFF Dakota Cassidy, whose name I used for my heroine and who loves the tea as much as I do, my mom, who helped take care of my mother-in-law so I could work, and to my husband and kid who provided me with Diet Cokes and apple pies from McDonalds as writerly fuel.

To my Rebels, you all RAWK! You keep me going every day with your support. I love you to the moon and back.

To my fans, I would not be anything without you. Seriously. If you keep reading, I'll keep writing! Thank you. Thank you. Thank you. If I were reviewing you all, you would get five-gazillion stars and a million-gazillion smooches.

Oh! And lest I forget, thank you strong, black coffee. Without you, I couldn't get out of bed in the morning, let alone write a single word.

BLURB

There are certain expectations when you grow up the oldest girl in a family of eleven. I'd always made a real effort to meet those demands and more. After all, I couldn't ask for better parents than Ruth and Ed Thompson. They didn't have a lot of money, but they made up for it in love and support. So, I was happy to do what I could to make their lives a little easier. Which meant, I didn't go out partying with my friends, I made good grades and graduated at the top of my class. I would run my younger brothers and sisters around and do errands for Mom and Dad. In other words, I never went through a rebellious phase, and I always tried to behave in a logical and rational manner. That is, until yesterday, when I decided to throw caution to the wind, for once, and act impulsively.

But now that I've awakened next to a dead body as the chill of spring rain seeps into my flesh, I am questioning every decision I've made since the full moon.

When a pack of werewolves move into her hometown of Peculiar, Missouri, good girl Dakota Thompson finds bad-boy werewolf Cal Rivers irresistible. The problem? She's a deer shifter. Who ever heard of a prey animal falling for a predator? Good girls avoid bad boys. Right?

Cal Rivers wants to make a real go in the Ozarks shifter community, but most folks are deeply suspicious of the werewolves—with one exception. The beautiful doe shifter Dakota Thompson. Cal finds himself drawn to the gorgeous and smart Dakota. In a mate kind of a way. But then he gets into it with Dakota's overprotective ex-boyfriend, which doesn't make him any new friends.

After a full moon, when everyone in town shifts and spends the night in their animal forms, Dakota wakes up next to the dead, mutilated body of her ex. The tense situation between the werewolves and the town's shifters go from precarious to catastrophic as Cal becomes one of the prime suspects in the murder. Together, Dakota and Cal work to find the real murderer to prevent an all-out war between predators and prey. Unfortunately, the killer isn't done yet...

PROLOGUE

ecember 20, 2018...the day before Chavvah and Billy Bob Smith's wedding.

"What do you think they want, Dakota?" Jo Jo Corman, a long-time family friend and my sister Michele's some-times boyfriend, asked as he leaned forward from the middle seat of my parent's cargo van to gawk at the herd of lycanthrope milling around the Smith yard. "It seems weird them showing up out of the blue."

"Well, it is Doc Smith's people, family, whatever," I said, placing the van in park. In the back, we had a stack of forty-six metal folding chairs. Brady Corman brought the folding tables on his truck, and Mom had swung by Blonde Bear Cafe and Sunny's Outlook to pick up the food. I peered out at the unusually tall gathering. "They're probably just here for the wedding."

Luke Dwyer, who sat in the passenger seat, shook his head. "Folks are already talking around town. They're nervous." Luke was everything I could want in a guy, nice, smart, and from a good family. His handsome, narrow face and large wide brown eyes marked him as a deer shifter like me. Plus, when we went out, he treated me with respect. Sometimes, though, his ideas about humans and outsiders verged on speciest.

"People are always afraid of the unknown," I said. And these wolves were the biggest unknown Peculiar had seen in quite a long time. Frankly, the last time they'd welcomed strangers, two of them had turned out to be serial killers who thought they could skinwalk if they took the right hide. It had turned out that they believed the right hide was Chavvah Trimmel, their first and last mistake. My brother Tyler was a sheriff's deputy, so he'd given me some of the nitty gritty. Basically, enough to give me nightmares. I shuddered as I recalled the way he'd described Mike Wares skinless corpse.

From the passenger seat, Luke shook his head as he stared at the newcomers. He took out his cellphone, slid his finger in a scribbly pattern across the front to unlock it, and started to take pictures of the group. "Hopefully, they're just passing through. The last thing we need in Peculiar is a bunch of werewolves taking our jobs and using up our resources. We're a small town. Lots of folks have had to get jobs in Lake Ozarks to make ends meet." He gripped my knee and gave it a squeeze. "Right, D?"

I shrugged. "I don't know. Doc Smith is a lycan, and he's pretty great."

2

Luke laughed. "The doc is awesome. I don't count him in with the rest of them."

My mom knocked at the window and saved me from the direction of this awful conversation. "Can you all give me a hand with the warmers? Or are you planning to hang out in the van all day?"

"Is that an option?" Jo Jo asked.

"You're not too old to spank, Jolon Corman," she said, using his given name.

He laughed. And with more interest, he asked, "Is that an option?"

"Young man!" Mom said, her eyes wide as she let out a hardy guffaw.

"What is going on out here?" Sunny Trimmel, one of my mom's best friends, asked. She wore both her children like saddlebags on either side of her hips. Jude, her oldest, stuck a wet finger in her ear. Sunny made an awful face and gently swatted his little hand away. Jude giggled, and I grinned.

Luke leaned to my ear. "You've got baby fever, huh?" he whispered.

I modeled Sunny and swatted him away. "Don't be stupid." I heard Jo Jo chuckling as I grabbed the door handle to escape a conversation I didn't even want to joke about. "You boys get the chairs out of the van, and I'll help Mom with the food."

"You got it," Jo Jo said.

I breathed a sigh of relief as I put distance between Luke and myself. I would have to end things with him and soon. He almost dropped the L-word on me last night, but I'd managed to change the subject quickly before he could actually say it. I'd stuck it out because my mom had been excited when I'd started dating Luke, but I couldn't be with someone who made me dread intimacy, even if we were "perfect for each other" as my mom had put it.

Mom approached and put her arm around me. "You okay?"

"Fine." I faked a smile. My feelings for Luke were luke-warm. In the beginning, there had been a little spark, and I'd thought, with enough time, I could fan it into a flame, but it had disappeared, smothered by the lack of oxygen. "I'm just feeling a little claustrophobic this morning."

She tilted her head to the side, waiting for me to elaborate. When I didn't, she patted my shoulder. "Let's get the food set up before it gets cold."

"Can I help?" The low, gruff voice startled me. I craned my gaze upward, because the guy had to be at least six-feet four-inches tall. Rays of sunlight scattered through his blond hair, highlighting the odd strand like tinsel. His blue eyes were darkened by shadows as he stared down at me.

"I...I, uhm," I stammered as my knees went all wobbly.

My mother, oblivious to the fact that I was about to have

a lust-induced stroke, said, "Sure. Grab those pans of eggs. They're the heaviest. What's your name?"

"Cal Rivers, ma'am," the guy said as he gave my mom a nod.

"I'm Ruth Thompson and this is my daughter, Dakota. Welcome to Peculiar, Cal."

"It's nice to meet you, Mrs. Thompson." He turned to me. "Dakota."

Heat crept into my cheeks. I grabbed the pan of bacon.

Sunny, thank heavens, walked over. "The tables are set up, and the lycans are helping Luke and Jo Jo set up the chairs. Let's get the food over there before people start eating their neighbors."

Cal laughed, and the sound stirred a deep longing inside me. No. No. No. First, he changed into a wolf on the full moon while I became a deer, a wolf's go to meal, and the thought brought me some relief from my sudden big, bad wolf fantasies. I handed a pan of bacon to Cal.

"I can take more," he said. So, I stacked a pan of sausage on top of it.

Luke strolled over. "Chairs and tables are set up. What's the hold up on the food?"

"No hold up." I averted my gaze from Cal.

Luke sized up Cal before glancing at me. I'd never been so glad that there was no such thing as a mind reader. I looked up, and Sunny was eyeballing me with the hint of a smirk on her face. I pressed my lips into a frown.

Okay, so I was glad that Luke wasn't a mind reader.

Numbly, I grabbed the pan of pancakes and followed Cal, Luke, my mom, and Sunny to the tables, and I couldn't keep my eyes off Cal's firm butt as he placed the eggs on the serving table.

Sunny caught up with me. She nudged me with her elbow. "That boy has a delicious booty." I gave her a startled look, and she giggled. "Watch your feet."

"What--ahh!" I careened forward in a lurch, desperate to keep the pancakes from flying out of my hands. With one hand, Cal grabbed the pan and with the other, he caught me around the waist, bringing my stumbling to a stop. Then Luke was grabbing me, and suddenly, I felt as if I were in a tug-o-war between them.

Cal let go first, Luke didn't have the right kind of hold on me, and I almost fell again.

Cal, who'd handed off the pancakes to someone, took a hold of my arms and righted me. "Are you okay?" he asked.

"Uhm, yes. I think I am. Thanks." I let slip a hint of a smile. I'm pretty sure I even batted my eyelashes. Gah!

"Good." He smiled back. "I'm glad."

I took a deep breath the quell the flutter in my belly.

Luke yanked me backward. I yelped and fell against him, my head hitting his chin.

"Mercy, Luke!" I staggered away from him. "What the heck?"

"Sorr--sorry, D." He reached out to me, his bottom lip bleeding. I took another step back. "I didn't mean--"

I rubbed the top of my head where we'd collided and glared at him. "I'm fine."

"You should have the doc look at your head, maybe get some ice for it," Cal said. He touched the spot. "You already have a bump."

"Quit touching my girl, asshole," Luke said.

"I'm just concerned." Cal nodded at Luke's lip. "You should get looked at, too." He grabbed a napkin from the table and held it out for Luke. "Here. You have some blood."

Luke slapped the napkin away. "Back off!"

A surge of fury, something I'd rarely felt, welled inside me. Jo Jo stood behind Luke, ready to back his play, and some very imposing lycanthropes crowded behind Cal.

"Stop it," I said. "All of you, just stop."

Chavvah jumped between Cal and Luke, Doc Smith on her heels. "What in the world is going on?" she asked, casting an accusing glance at Cal.

"Luke is completely overreacting. I tripped over a rock,

and all this guy did was keep me from landing on my face." Not to mention the pancakes.

"Don't be stupid, D. He has been eyeballing you since we got here. He probably tripped you himself."

My mom snapped her fingers at Luke. "Lucas Dwyer, I'll thank you not to call my daughter stupid. Now." She pointed to the van. "Go. Home."

Cal, whose veins were popping from his forehead, leaned in. "Yeah, Lucas. Go. Home."

Chavvah snapped her fingers at Cal, mimicking my mom's action. "There's no call to make things worse."

His face hardened then relaxed. "Sorry, ma'am," he said to Chav. "I don't know what came over me."

I looked back once as my mom escorted me into Chavvah and Doc Smith's house. Cal gave me a quick nod. I nodded back then went inside.

Mom spoke to me confidentially once we were away from prying ears. "Don't be too hard on Luke. Men in love can be a little hot headed, my girl. Remember the in-love part when you're ready to forgive him."

Her words sunk inside me like a weighted burden. I didn't want him to be in love with me. How could he possibly love someone who couldn't love him back? I wanted to say as much, but the hopeful look on my mother's face stopped me short of the truth. "I will, Mom."

"You might want to steer clear of the wolves while you're

at it," she added. "No sense in adding fuel to the fire." She gave my cheek a pat. "I'm so glad I don't have to worry about you."

"Nope." Though, I wished like crazy someone would worry about me, because worrying about myself had become a serious chore.

CHAPTER ONE

I woke up with my cheek pressed against soft, fragrant dirt. The dank, earthy smell mixed with the sharp scent of shortleaf pine told me my location. I rolled onto my back and blinked up at the gray sky.

I had stick and twigs poking through my hair and my feet were covered in mud. "Dakota Thompson," I muttered, "what did you do last night?"

Hard to know. Most shifters didn't wake up with memories of their moonlit jaunts after the first full moon of the month. Our animal forms, during forced transformations like last night, processed experiences so differently our human brains couldn't translate. In other words, I had no idea what my doe-self did last night.

Dark clouds blocked out the early morning sun, muting the colors of the surrounding woods. It was unusually quiet, and I allowed myself to enjoy the peace for a few seconds. I was the oldest of nine children, and I still lived with my parents. I helped them at home and worked for our family business, Doe Run Automotive. Living in a house with eight other people, silence was a rare commodity. A slight breeze brushed over my skin. If it hadn't been so cool out, I would have called the humidity tropical, but since it was only fifty degrees, judging by the goosebumps on my arms, the dampness in the air made it feel more like forty. My transition bag hung in the ancient oak where my doe always ended up during this time of the lunar cycle. Most shifters woke up in the same area every month. This small clearing near the giant oak happened to be my spot. My mother told me it was nature's way of keeping therianthropes safe during the full moon.

Before I could get up to dress, a rustling of dried leaves drew my attention. I popped to my feet and froze, my emotions a mixture of horror and admiration as I realized who stood directly across from me. An extremely naked and, uhm, well-endowed Adonis by the name of Cal Rivers, one of the new wolves who had come to Peculiar. Turns out that one of our own, Chavvah Smith, was their new leader. The group had moved into town in December and was currently living in Peculiar on probationary terms. It had not been a smooth transition for the wolf shifters. While the town had embraced Dr. Billy Bob Smith, previously the only lycanthrope in town, as one of their own, having a whole pack of wolves show up had brought on prejudices based in the fear of the unknown.

For the first two full moons since their arrival, many of the parents in town had kept their families locked in "just in case". My family had made a point of going out and running, like we normally did. It wasn't like we didn't have other predators in town. We were a mixed bag of therianthropes in Peculiar, and the doc and Chavvah had given their assurances that the wolves would stay away from therian groups on those nights. As a matter of fact, part of the town council's approval of the lycanthropes staying in Peculiar was that they stayed on the Smith property during the full moon. I'd overheard Mom talking to Chavvah and Sunny about it. Since all shifters turned to the baser animal selves on the first full moon, Chavvah promised, with the help of her spirit guide, Brother Wolf, that the lycans would strictly adhere to their probationary contract. Since some people in town weren't happy about the new arrivals, the agreement was the only thing keeping the peace.

Even so, I could sense a nervous tension in my parents when we went out in January not normally present. But this was the third full moon since their arrival, and the first two had came and went without any issues. So, what was Cal doing here in the prey animal territory?

"It is Dakota, right?" he asked. The smooth, low tones of his voice sent a thrill through me.

"Yes," I confirmed. "I remember you. You're Cal Rivers." I'd first laid eyes on him the day before Chavvah and Doc Smith's wedding. My ex-boyfriend Luke Dwyer, who'd I'd broken up with at the end of December, had started a fight with Cal because he didn't like the way the wolf had looked at me. But I had liked it just fine. As a matter of fact, I hadn't been able to stop thinking about Cal since. I'd seen him around a couple of times, but even though Peculiar was small, it wasn't so tiny that chance encounters happened all the time. Regardless of my feelings, the werewolf shouldn't have been *here*. My family ran on Tom Hackenstraw's property on the full moon just southwest of town, a hundred-acre area reserved for the non-predator animals. Non-predator being the word of the day. This guy, especially the way he was looking at me, definitely fell into the predator category.

A brisk breeze stirred my hair over my face, and I finger combed it out of my eyes. "What are you doing here?"

He gave me a crooked smile. "I think I'm a little lost. Where is here?" He ran his large, callused hands through his thick, sandy-colored hair.

Therianthropes weren't uncomfortable with nudity, after all, clothes didn't magically reappear when we shifted back to human, but everything about Cal made me self-conscious. He was a werewolf, and up until his group had shown up to town in December, my only experience with lycanthropes was Doctor Smith, so my knowledge was limited.

The way Cal stood in front of me without even a token attempt at covering up told me he wasn't self-conscious at all. And why would he be? His body was rocking hot.

I focused on keeping my eyes at his chest level as I sat down, giving him side view only, and pulled my knees to my chest. "You are on the opposite side of town from where you're supposed to be."

The corner of his mouth quirked up in a half-smile that I found charming. "I must have taken a wrong turn somewhere."

"You sure did," Lukas Dwyer said as he entered the clearing. He looked from Cal to me. "Are you okay, D?"

Ugh. I squeezed my knees tighter. "Yep. I'm ooh-key doh-key." My parents seriously approved of Luke. He filled all the requirements of a good girl's boyfriend. His dad, Jonathan Dwyer, owned the local grocery store where Luke worked as the manager. Good job. *Check.* Mr. Dwyer had been a friend of my parents in high school. Good background. *Check.* Mr. Dwyer had met his wife, an integrator, which was another word for therianthropes who were raised among humans, when he'd gone away to college. Both were deer shifters. Good genes. *Check.* Problem was, I didn't feel any sizzle and heat when I looked at him. *Uncheck. Uncheck. Uncheck.*

Not like I felt when I looked at Cal. I glanced at the lycan through my lashes. He vibrated with an intense energy. I bet he was all kinds of naughty. He must've seen me checking him out because he flashed me a grin that I read as: You bet I am.

I swallowed hard and cast my gaze elsewhere.

Luke grabbed my bag from where it hung and handed it

to me. Luke's chest puffed out as he glared at Cal. "Do you mind?" he snapped.

The posturing irritated the crap out of me. I wasn't an object to be possessed and Luke's attitude made me bristle, especially since we were no longer a couple. "Excuse me. Would you both leave so I can get dressed without an audience?"

Cal lowered his eyes. "I apologize if I caused you any distress. It was not my intention." With a quick nod, he shimmered, hair sprouting along his skin, his body reshaping until he was in the form of a large, gray wolf. He locked gazes with me, his ice blue eyes startling against the dark gray fur around his eyes.

Then he turned and loped away.

"The nerve of that jack ass," Luke said. "I'm going to report him to the town council about this. He shouldn't be anywhere near here this morning."

I cast Luke an annoyed glance. "Just drop it. No one is hurt, and he left of his own accord."

"Why are you defending him?"

The hair on the back of my neck bristled. "I'm not defending him. I just don't understand why you're so eager to ruin other people. The lycanthropes have not gotten into any trouble since they arrived in town. Please don't be the reason they get thrown out. Don't be that guy."

Luke shook his head. "Sorry, D. But he broke the rules. The ones they agreed to."

"The werewolf isn't the only guy who shouldn't be here. I told you it was over. So why come?" I asked as I pulled my shirt over my head.

"Don't be like that. We're good together."

"I can't be with someone who goes out of his way to hurt someone else."

"That's not fair."

"Maybe not, but it's the way I feel. I don't want to see you anymore. Now, go, so I can finish getting dressed." In a way, I agreed with Luke. It wasn't fair. I wished I could magically find him attractive, but I didn't, but one look from Cal revved my engines to full throttle. I'd never had that same kind of reaction to Luke. *Good girls don't date werewolves,* I told myself firmly. But I couldn't date Luke, either.

Once my ex was gone, I dressed quickly. I scanned the woods for more therians. Unfortunately, as a deer shifter, my eyes were no better than a human's. Worse in some respects, because I, like most my species, was mildly red-green color blind. However, my sense of smell was pretty damned good, and I could still detect the faint aroma of Cal's dense fur and musk. He hadn't been in wolf form long, so how was the scent of him so strong, and why did I know to my core that it was him and not some other shifter? How long had he been lying near me before I

17

awakened? I pulled my hair into a pony tail, and the scent became even more potent.

I sniffed my palms. My stomach dipped as I inhaled deeply. My hands... they were covered in the werewolf's scent.

CHAPTER TWO

I'd traveled straight home from the woods and right up to my room in an effort to avoid conversation. My mom had a way of making people want to talk even when they didn't feel like it. I worried what would happen to Cal and the other wolves if Luke decided to report him for being in a prey area after the full moon. Would the town council really force all thirty-seven were-wolves to leave town? Would Chavvah and Doc Smith go with them? Our town would be ten-kinds of awful without both of them here. Was this my fault? After all, I'd had to come into contact with Cal shortly after I turned back this morning, during twilight, that moment when my animal consciousness left my body and my human consciousness returned. Otherwise, my hands wouldn't smell like him.

I clenched my hands to my sides and made a real effort not to sniff them again, but what did it say about me that

I hadn't washed them, yet, either. I was a mess, that's what.

"Hey, Kota," my youngest brother Linus said. He leaned his slender hip against the frame of my open bedroom door and ran his fingers through his buff-blond hair. "Can you take me to baseball practice after school today?"

I smiled at Linus. "Sure, squirt." He had grown two inches over the school year, but he was still small for a twelve-year-old.

He grinned. "You're the best." He took off down the hall toward the stair. "Mom!" I heard him holler. "Dakota said she'd take me to practice!"

A minute later, mom poked her head in the door. "Don't forget you are closing this afternoon for your dad and me. We have a town council meeting we have to attend."

"I haven't forgotten. I'll only be gone for about forty minutes or so. Linus gets out of school at three-fifteen. I'll have him dropped off by three-forty-five. That leaves me plenty of time to get back to the garage by four."

She walked over to me and kissed my forehead. "Thanks, baby girl. You're a life saver." She smelled of vanilla, cinnamon, and freshly peeled apples.

I took a moment to enjoy the aroma then said, "Whatever you need, Mom. You know that."

My parents had nine children, and they worked hard to provide for us. My older brother Tyler had moved out at eighteen when he married his high school sweetheart, and Taylor had moved out to go to college the same year. When he came back, he'd rented an apartment, and now he owned his own home. I didn't begrudge either of them, but their absence left it to me to help Mom and Dad with the day-to-day running of the house and the business. Michele, who was twenty-two, two years younger than me, helped out sometimes, but she'd made a tidy little business out of baby-sitting. Between Sunny Trimmel's and Willy Boden's kids, she kept pretty busy.

My phone dinged. I picked it up from my nightstand. I had a text message from an unfamiliar number. It said, *I'm sorry about this morning. Will you let me buy you lunch to make up for it?*

Who is this? I texted back, though the way my heart raced, I was pretty certain I already knew the answer.

Cal. Sorry. Should have led with my name.

I typed, *How did you get my number?*

Your sister Michele.

Of course. Michele would have no qualms handing out my number to a hot werewolf. She thought Luke was as boring as dry toast, and I didn't disagree with her. I looked at the phone's display. It was ten-fifteen. *It's a little early for lunch, don't you think?* All the same, I wanted to talk to him, if for no other reason than to warn him about Luke, but the idea of meeting with him made me nervous.

Then how about dessert? he asked. *Sunny's Outlook makes some pretty good cinnamon rolls.*

Sunny's made great cinnamon rolls. I know, because I'd helped them several times over the past couple of years when Sunny and Chav had been short of help, and I'd eaten a lion's share of their desserts. Still, I couldn't miss the opportunity to brag about the best dessert in town. I smiled. *Not as good as my mom's apple pie.*

Are you inviting me over for apple pie?

"Are you texting with Luke?" Mom asked.

I pressed the face of my phone to my chest, and Mom gave me a weird look. I hadn't told her that I had broken things off with Luke. I was pretty sure she and Luke's mom had planned our wedding along with our next twenty years when they'd found out we were dating. "Uhm, why do you think I'm talking to him?"

"Baby girl, you are practically glowing. I remember what it was like to be young and in love." Her large brown eyes brightened. "Only, your father used to write me notes." She smirked. "Some of them were very naughty."

"Oh." I held up my hand in a stop motion. "No, Mom. Just no."

She giggled. "You know, I'm just happy your happy again."

"What do you mean?"

"A mom knows when her child is down. You don't have to

tell me what happened between the two of you. I'm just glad you've managed to get it sorted out. You are happy, right?"

She looked at me with such love, I couldn't bring myself to tell her the truth about Luke and me. "I'm happy."

"Do you want to come down and help me do some baking?"

I peeked at my phone then shook my head. "I'm going to go into town for a little bit if you don't mind."

"You tell Luke I said hello."

"Okay," I said, the word thick in my throat. I never lie to my mom. That wasn't me. Ever. And, while technically, I hadn't told her that Luke was the one texting me, she'd taught me well enough that a lie of omission was still a lie. "Mom..."

She tilted her head. "What is it, sweetheart?"

How could I tell her about Cal? Especially, since, at this point, there wasn't really anything to tell.

"Do you need me to pick up anything for you while I'm in town?" I finally asked.

"Yes, actually. Could you grab some flour and sugar from the grocery store?"

My stomach clenched. Since Luke's family owned the Dwyer Fresh Market, it was the last place I wanted to go.

"Sure, Mom. I'll pick that up for you." Great. Maybe I'd get lucky, and Luke wouldn't be at the store. If I ran into him, I could always just say I had to run an errand for Mom.

My phone buzzed. *Pie or cinnamon rolls?*

"I'll let you get back to sexting."

"Mom!"

She wiggled her brows at me. "You're young, Dakota. It's okay to act like it."

Thank heavens she left my doorway before I could respond. As I stared at the screen, I gripped my phone tight enough to make my fingertips ache.

After a few seconds of internal debating, I texted Cal back.

Cinnamon rolls. Maybe lunch if you play your cards right. One hour.

I'll bring the whole deck, he replied.

GUILT NIGGLED AT ME, as I searched the baking aisle for self-rising flour...just not enough to make me change my mind about meeting Cal at Sunny's Outlook. I'd left the house a little early, so I could stop by the grocery first. I rationalized that if I ran into Luke, I could tell him I'd come to town to run an errand for mom, and it wouldn't be a total lie.

"Can I help you?" a man asked.

I turned and saw one of the store's employees, a guy named Jack Trevors. Jack had been an integrator before moving to town a few years back. He was tall, lanky, with brown hair and dark eyes. I knew of him, but I didn't know him.

"You all seem to be out of white flour. Unless, I'm just blind, which might very well be the case." But I'd traveled up and down the aisle twice and couldn't find it.

"Sorry, miss. We're out of stock right now. Supposed to get some more in tomorrow." He pointed at a whole wheat flour and said, "Will that work?"

"Only if I'm trying to upset my mother. She's particular about her pie crusts, and that wholesome stuff is not going to cut it for her."

"D!" I fought back a groan as Luke walked toward me. "What are you doing here?"

"Mom needed flour for baking, but you all seem to be out."

He furrowed his brow. "I signed the new shipment of dry goods in from Springfield about an hour ago. It should be in the back. I'll go get you one."

"I don't want to be any trouble."

He smiled at me, as if we hadn't been arguing first thing this morning. "It's no trouble for you."

"Thanks."

Jack said, "I'll go get it."

"No," Luke told him. "I'll get it. I need you in the deli. Marcus just took a break, and I need someone on the slicer."

"Are you sure, Luke?" Jack said. "I'll can bring it up."

An ugly look of annoyance passed over Luke's face before he said, "You didn't even know it had come in. Pathetic. Besides, I need you in the deli."

Jack put up his fingers. "You got it, Mr. Dwyer," he said angrily.

I looked at the many flavors of frosting while I waited. I bet the coconut pecan frosting tasted really good with a spoon and nothing else. The double whipped chocolate fudge sounded delicious as well. I counted twenty different flavors. I could easily make my own smorgasbord out of the bunch.

"Here you go," Luke said, handing me a five-pound bag. "Is this the one you want?"

"That's exactly what she wants," I said. When I accepted the bag from him, a dusting of loose flour sprinkled my jeans and my brown boots. "Shoot."

Luke reached down and swiped at my pants with his

hand.

I stepped back from him. "It's okay."

He frowned. "Tell me what I need to do, D. I'll do what it takes to win you back."

What he didn't understand was he'd never won me in the first place. There was nothing to get back. "I'm not a prize to be collected or had, Luke." I put the flour in my grocery basket. "I'm sorry I hurt you, but it would be crueler to lead you on."

"I can't believe you'd prefer that Neanderthal of a were-wolf to me."

"That's not why I broke up with you."

He snorted derisively. "Whatever. I have invested a lot of time in you. In us. We are perfect for each other. Why can't you see that?"

"Stop it, Luke."

"I'll tell you what," he rubbed my cheek with his thumb. "I won't report the lycanthrope for being off the Smith property if you come out with me tonight. Just one night and your boyfriend and his kind won't have to worry about me getting them kicked out."

I moved his hand away. "I can't stop you from doing what you're going to do, Luke, but maybe I'll tell the council you're jealous so your making up lies." I wouldn't. At least, I didn't think I would. But the thought of Cal being kicked out of town because my ex was a jerk who couldn't let go made me ache.

He shook his head. "You wouldn't." He leaned toward me. "All you have to do is go out with me. Jackson Smart is having a party tonight."

"On a Thursday?"

"Every night is a weekend when you're the boss," he joked. "Come on. Say you'll go."

I'd never been to any of the parties out at Jackson's new place. I heard they could get wild. Michele had stumbled home a night or two after one of his shindigs, but the idea of crowds of people, being forced to socialize with drunken yahoos, well, it lacked any appeal for me. "I'm sorry, Luke. The answer is no."

"So, this is it? We're done?"

Yes! I thought. For the second time today. Why was he holding onto the idea of us so tightly? "You know this can't work between us. I'm not sure it ever did."

His fingers curled into fists as he quietly asked, "And what about your wolfman?"

In a moment of really bad timing, Cal Rivers walked around the corner. My eyes widened. Luke must have seen something on my face because he whipped around and cast and accusing glare at Cal. I reached out to stop Luke as he moved a step in the werewolf's direction.

He rounded on me. "Him? I can't believe you dumped me for that guy?"

"No," I told him. "I didn't break up with you because of him."

Luke huffed. "Yeah, right. Things were fine with us, D, until he showed up in December. You have been pulling away from me ever since."

I shook my head. "If you had really been paying attention, you'd have noticed much sooner than December." Though meeting Cal had brought home just how much I didn't want to be with Luke.

He surprised me by grabbing my upper arms and yanking me toward him. "You can't do this, Dakota. Please, don't do this to me. To us."

"You shouldn't put your hands on a lady," Cal said, now only a few feet away and closing in fast, his voice calm and monotone.

"I'm fine," I said calmly. I met Luke's gaze. "We're fine. Right? Luke was just about to let me go."

"What is going on here?" my dad said, coming up the aisle behind me. Crap, I needed to get out of here before anyone else showed up to witness my humiliation.

Upon seeing my dad, Luke instantly dropped his hands to his side, and I stepped away from him.

"Nothing is going on here, Mr. Thompson," Luke said.

But my dad was not a stupid man. While it might seem like deer shifters would be one of the more diplomatic of therianthropes, bucks were known for being fiercely protective of their young. I got a bad feeling he was about to show Luke the sharp end of his antlers.

"Hey, Dad. What are you doing here?" I asked.

"Picking up some soda for the shop. Now, you better answer my question?" He stared at Luke.

"We were just having a conversation," Luke said.

"You always talk with your hands, son?"

I heard a slight growl coming from Cal. The skin on my cheeks tightened as I grimaced. I tugged at the collar of my shirt. "Is it getting warm in here?"

My dad glanced at Cal. "What's your part in all this?"

Cal shrugged. "I'm just here for beef jerky."

"It's two aisles down," Luke snarled.

The weight of Dad's gaze fell on me. He was a thin man with delicate features, typical of deer therians, but in this moment, he'd made himself large and imposing. "Give me your basket and get on out of here, girl. I'll take the flour home to your ma."

"She wants sugar, too."

He raised a brow. "I'll grab it on my way out. Now you go before someone says or does something he might regret." My dad's eyes pivoted between the two men.

"Yes, sir." My ears burned as I nodded. I handed the basket to Dad and fled the scene without looking back.

Damn it. I'd really made a mess of things the way I'd handled Luke and Cal. If I had quit things with Luke after our first few dates, I wouldn't be having this problem now. In hindsight, it would have been the responsible thing to do, but at the time, I really thought I could eventually develop feelings for him. On paper, he was the perfect suitor. He ticked all the boxes. But real life didn't come down to checks and balances. I had no chemistry with Luke, and the fact that he thought we did made me feel even guiltier.

I practically ran toward the exit but was stopped in my path by Mary Ann Dwyer, Luke's mother. She wore her hair in a high chignon, reminding me of a blond Audrey Hepburn. "Dakota," she said with so much feeling it made my teeth ache. She reached out to me, her cherry red nails perfectly manicured as always, sparkling under the bright artificial lights.

I reluctantly took her hands. "Hi, Mrs. Dwyer."

"It's so good to see you. When are you coming over again? I keep telling Luke to invite you for dinner, but I'm afraid my invitation isn't being passed along."

"I..." I closed my mouth, unsure of what to say. Obviously, Luke had been as quiet about our break up with his parents as I had been with mine. It was time for them to know the truth. "Luke and I aren't seeing each other anymore," I said.

Her pleasant expression changed to one of confusion and hurt. "I hadn't heard."

Before she could get mad at my mom, I added, "We really haven't told anyone. Not even my parents."

Mary Ann nodded. "I'm sorry to hear this. You were...good for him."

"I'm sorry, too." My pulse jumped a notch as I waited for her to process my revelation. I needed to get out of the store. "I have to go, Mrs. Dwyer. It was lovely to see you."

"And you," she said absently then walked away.

When I finally made it outside, I let go of the breath I'd been holding. My phone dinged.

We still on for cinnamon rolls?

I stared at the screen, trying to will myself to tell him no. He was the wrong sort for me. While therians could date across species of animals, it was still rare for predators and prey animals to mix romantically. I'd never heard of anyone eating a spouse on a full moon, but it didn't mean it couldn't happen.

Better not, I texted. Then added, *another time, maybe?*

My heart was in my throat as I watched the moving ellipses on the screen as Cal texted his response. The dots stopped then started again. Then stopped.

Finally, he texted back. *Meet me tonight. Let's run together...again.*

Again? Had we run together last night? It would explain why I smelled like his fur, but the idea of a wolf and deer hanging out on a full moon created more questions than it answered.

I imagined him anticipating my text in the same way I had. After a short moment of trying to talk myself out of doing something stupid, I gave into temptation.

Tonight. But not in Peculiar.

CHAPTER THREE

I gripped the steering wheel in my pick up, my nails digging into the leather wrap as I raced to the school. I'd occupied my hands rebuilding a two-barrel carburetor Dad had pulled off an 88' Chevy truck this afternoon while my mind had raced over the morning's events. So much so, that I nearly forgot I was supposed to pick Linus up for practice. When I pulled into the parking lot, my brother waved, his expression awash with relief at my arrival. My truck nosedived when I applied the brakes too hard, reminding me I needed to look at the front suspension soon. Also, the outer handle on my passenger door was broken, so I'd reached over and opened it from the inside for him. He threw his ball bag in the back of the truck then climbed in.

"Hey, bug," I said to him. "Sorry, I'm late."

"Took you long enough," he quipped. "You need to fix your door."

"I'm too busy running little brothers to baseball practice," I countered. Though he wasn't wrong. I did need to fix the door, and the frontend suspension, and replace the exhaust manifold which was causing a ticking sound when I revved the engine. Unfortunately, I didn't have the money for the parts I needed, or frankly, the time.

"Mechanic heal thyself."

"Har har," I told him. "Hilarious. If you don't eventually wind up in jail for indecent exposure, you should become a comedian." My youngest brother was a bit of an exhibitionist. He preferred four legs over two, and since our clothing doesn't shift with us, all of us Thompsons, even my other siblings, always kept a spare shirt and a pair of pants handy just in case Linus decided to publicly transform back to human after a run.

"You know..." He gave me a sly side-eye glance. "...I considered running there on my own."

"Better to keep your clothes on." He was geared up for baseball, with the stirrup pants, a t-shirt, and cleats. I knocked the hard-plastic athletic cup he wore in his pants with the back of my knuckle, and said, "Hard to protect your balls from a fast pitch when you're naked."

"Kota!" He tried to smack my hand, but I moved to fast for him to catch me.

"Missed me," I said on a laugh before sobering the conversation. "Point is, you have to be more careful, kid. Especially now that your antlers are growing points. You can't show up anywhere outside of town as a deer. First, you never know if you might run into a human. Second, poachers are real, and they won't hesitate to shoot a young buck like yourself. You have to keep yourself safe."

"I know. Sheesh. I was joking. I'm not going to expose myself outside of town."

"You know, there's a lot of people who wish you'd stop exposing yourself in town."

"I meant my other nature." He gave me a sly smile. "But, I do like it breezy."

Peculiar School district was listed as private, not public education, and the sports fields had been built north of town, beyond the one bridge in and out of Peculiar, and near a small gas station ran by a raccoon shifter named Pete Shephard, to keep the humans from nosing around. For many of us living in a therianthrope town, these sporting events had been our first contact with humans. Good practice at blending in, my mom would say, for when we went off to college.

I'd never had a desire to sit in a college classroom. I hadn't liked high school much at all. I had always found it easier to learn by doing. I think that even if my parents hadn't owned an auto shop, I probably would have found another way to work with my hands. I glanced at my nailbeds. They were darkened in the creases with old carburetor fluid residue, and my fingers and palms were rough and callused.

When we came up on the field there were eight vehicles, five trucks and two cars, parked in the lot. Ten boys around Linus's age were already out on the diamond throwing balls around. Coach Denny Johnson, Elbert Johnson's oldest son, was working with Levi Smart, Mark Smart's youngest son and one of Linus's best friends, on his pitching. Linus played catcher, and his face reflected his panic at being late, as he jumped out of the truck as soon as I stopped. He grabbed his gear and ran to where the coach and Levi were warming up without so much as a goodbye to me.

"You're welcome," I muttered. It was a little after four now, and my parents needed to get to their meeting, which meant I was going to make everyone late today. Mom called about the time I got back on the road. "Hey," I said. "I just dropped Linus off, and I'm heading to the shop now."

"Can you swing by Doc Smith's before you come back into town. Lisa Ann cut her arm on some barbwire. I called ahead, and Doc will have some salve ready for you when you get there."

"How did she cut herself on barbwire?" We didn't have any fences like that near town.

"She and Bobby Davis decided to go check out Robyn Smith's fainting goats." Robyn was a squirrel shifter, so no relation to the doctor. "She'd put some barbwire up after one of her goats got killed by a wild animal last summer. Darn fool kid. I've grounded her for a month."

"Bobby?" Bobby Davis was a mountain lion shifter, and at fourteen, he already had a reputation for trouble.

Mom chuckled. "You let me worry about who your sister hangs out with."

"Okay. I have my key if you want to lock up the shop when you go."

"Thanks, baby," she said.

I put my blinker on for Doctor Smith's road. "I'm here at the doc's now. Talk later."

My truck bounced hard as I made my way down the gravel drive. Doc's medical office was adjacent to his home, and I wondered how that was working out for them now that they had a baby on the way. Chavvah, at three months, looked like she had stuffed a basketball under her maternity top.

Before I could get out of my truck, Kyle Avery and Karina Wells walked out of the clinic. Karina's eyes were red and puffy, and Kyle looked ready for a brawl. They were both Michele's age, but we'd all hung around together a time or two. I got out as they reached Kyle's car.

"Are you all right?" I asked Karina.

Kyle turned to glower at me, his face turning red as if just my presence pissed him off.

"Don't, Kyle," Karina said. She coughed out a choking sob when she tried to say more, and Kyle's expression softened. He opened the passenger door, and as angry as he appeared, he was surprisingly gentle as he helped her inside.

I heard her quietly plead with him, "Please. Please don't say anything."

Kyle nodded and told her, "I won't. I promise." His tightly clenched fists did not reflect the tenderness he used when he spoke to her. He gave her a kiss on the forehead then closed the door when she had her feet inside.

Karina lowered her window when he made his way around to the driver's side. She hiccupped then said, "Can you ask Michele to call me later?"

"Sure." I watched them go before I headed into the clinic.

I was surprised to see the silver haired, gray-eyed Etta Smith behind the counter. "Hi there," I said a little too brightly. I'd been curious about the volatile wolf since I'd seen her and Chavvah duke it out during some weird pre-wedding ritual. I hoped that her working for the doc meant they were on better terms. I'd overheard my mom talking with Sunny and Chav about her, and the words "anger issues" came up a lot.

"Hi," Etta said. "Do you have an appointment?"

"No, nothing like that. My mom, Ruth Thompson, said Doc Smith would have some salve waiting for me."

Etta cast her dark gaze down at the desk and picked up a small container. "Billy Bob told me to tell you to apply the ointment twice daily. It should heal it up in a few days."

"You know the secret ingredient in Doc's salves, right?"

Etta tilted her head to the side. "Spit," she said matter of factly. She cracked a smile after.

I giggled. "It's so gross, but so effective."

She laughed. "Right? I grew up around it as a cure all, and I still think it's gross."

"I'm Dakota," I told her.

"Etta," she replied. She handed me the small container. "Thanks."

"For what?"

"For lightening the mood. It's been like a morgue around here today."

"Did someone die?"

"No." She brushed her long hair away from her shoulders and shook her head. "Might as well, though. So much crying. I never knew a doctor's office could be so damn depressing."

"Well, people don't come here because they feel good."

Etta snorted, taking some of the shine off her perfect beauty, and it made me like her even more. "Truth," she said. "Billy Bob is pretty strict about patient confidentiality, as he should, so I can't say more, but man, I've had a day of it."

"How are you settling in? I hope nobody is giving you all a

hard time. Peculiar is a great place to grow up, but the locals can get a little cautious when it comes to outsiders."

Etta grinned, her gray eyes shining like silver under the fluorescent lighting. "Cautious is one word for it. I don't go into town much if I can help it. Although, I'm getting pretty stir crazy just hanging out here."

"Have you made any friends?"

"One," she said. She gave me a warm smile. "At least, I hope so."

I returned her warmth. "I'd like that." I pocketed the salve. "See you around."

"Sure," Etta said. "Don't be a stranger."

When I reached the door handle, I turned back on impulse. "Do you want to come over tonight for dinner? My mom is a great cook."

Etta blinked, frowned, then finally, she nodded, her smile suddenly shy. "That'd be real nice. Are you sure your mom won't mind?"

"What's one more mouth?"

Etta shrugged. "Okay then."

I wrote down the address on the back of a Doe Run Automotive business card for her. "Do you need a ride?"

"I'll find my way." She waved the card at me. "Thanks again for the invite. It will be good to get away from this place for a little while." The way she said it made me think that maybe things weren't as settled between her and her father as I initially assumed.

"Great. We eat at six."

"Awesome. I'll bring my appetite."

CHAPTER FOUR

"*H*and me the roasted garlic from the fridge," Mom said, as she whirled around the kitchen. She had a chuck roast braising in the oven, red-skinned potatoes boiled for garlic smashed potatoes, homemade cream corn she'd made from corn she'd cut off the cob last summer and had frozen. "While you're at it, dice me an onion."

Linus ran past the kitchen in full fur and hooves.

"Boy! You better get changed and dressed before company arrives," Mom ordered.

Her excitement level over hosting a dinner for Etta made me uncomfortable. "You know, just because she's the Doc's daughter doesn't mean you should meddle."

Mom shooed me with a quick wave of a hand towel. "I'm not planning to meddle. I am just happy you've reached out to her. Chav's been worried about the girl being lonely, and I want to make sure she feels welcome."

"It's dinner, Mom," Michele said, poking her head into the kitchen. "Don't make a big deal out of it or you'll scare her off." She smirked at me, and I rolled my eyes. I didn't say anything back, because in all honesty, I agreed with her.

"Go make sure your brother is dressed," Mom said to Michele. "And later you can tell me what you've been up to all day." She gave my younger sister and all-knowing-mom stare.

Michele blanched. "Going."

I had to walk fast to catch up with her in the living room. "Hey, Mishy. I ran into Kyle and Karina at the doctor's office today. Karina wanted you to call her."

Michele's expression darkened. "Okay."

"Bad news?" I asked.

"I can't talk about it, Kota. Sorry. Not yet." She looped her pinky into mine. "You're okay, right?"

"Yeah." I swallowed, my throat suddenly dry at her serious tone. "Fine. Why?"

"I know you've been struggling with boyfriend stuff, lately."

"How do you know?"

"Maybe Sunny's psychic ability is wearing off on me." She touched her nose and wiggled it. "Mostly, though, I've seen you decline several calls from him. He didn't...you know, hurt you or anything, did he?"

"I'm the one who did the hurting," I confessed. "I feel bad because I think he really loves me. I don't feel the same way. I've told him several times, but he doesn't seem to hear me when I say it's over."

She frowned. "Some guys don't like to take no for an answer. Luke is one of them." She squeezed my pinky tightly. "Be careful, okay?"

"Do you know something?"

"No." Michele shook her head. "Not really. It's a feeling."

"So, you really are turning psychic," I teased.

The doorbell rang, and Linus shifted from deer to human. Michele turned her attention from me to him. "Get your butt up the stairs, you little streaker!" She ran up after him.

"I've got the door, Mom," I yelled.

Etta stood out on the porch with a bouquet of yellow, blue, and purple spring flowers. I couldn't stop the chuckle that burbled up in my throat.

"What?" she asked, shaking the flowers. "It was this or wine, and I wasn't sure of your mom's policy on alcohol."

I ushered her inside. "Flowers were the right choice," I said confidentially. "Mom! Etta's here."

Mom rounded the corner, stripping her apron off, and

tucking loose strands of blonde hair behind her ears. "Oh, Etta. It's so nice to have you, dear. Come in." Her eyes widened when she saw the flowers. "How thoughtful? I'll take those and get them into some water."

My brother Butch bounded down the steps with Thomas on his heels, both their hair freshly washed and wearing suspiciously clean clothes. Uh oh. I didn't like the way they were eyeballing my new friend.

"Etta, these are my brothers Butch and Thomas." Butch was sixteen and Thomas was a year younger, which meant they were both in full hormonal bloom. "Ignore them if they get creepy."

"Kota!" Thomas protested.

Etta giggled, and it sounded weirdly girly coming from the tall, warrior chick who'd I'd watched fight Chavvah three months earlier. I liked it.

"It'll be another fifteen minutes before dinners ready," Mom said, coming back into the foyer, bouquet-free. "Dakota, baby, why don't you show Etta around. Introduce her to your brothers and sisters."

"She's already met Thing One and Thing Two." I jerked my thumb at my teenager brothers.

Both boys groaned.

Mom laughed. "Thomas and Butch, go tell Dad it's time to clean up for dinner. He's in the shop." She winked at Etta and me as my brothers hastily escaped the awkwardness. "Give them a break, Dakota. You remember what it was like to be that age."

"I really don't." I nodded to Etta and gestured to the stairs. "We can start with my room."

"Sounds great," she said.

I heard Michele down the hall, and I thought she was talking to Linus, until I heard her say, "Don't cry, Ree-ree," the nickname she called Karina, "I'll come over tonight after dinner. We'll talk more, okay?"

Linus came out of his room and slid in socked feet along the hardwood floors in the hall right past us. He let out a triumphant, "Yeah!"

I pointed as he skipped down the stairs. "That's my youngest brother Linus." I knocked outside Michele's room, and Etta and I stopped outside the door. "Michele, this is Etta Smith."

Michele set her phone down, her smile widening even though it didn't quite reach her eyes. "It's so nice to meet you. I've heard so much."

Etta frowned. "From who?"

"I babysit for Sunny Trimmel and Willy Boden. Those ladies talk like I'm not around most the time." Michele smiled. "Don't worry. It was mostly good."

"Don't mind her," I told Etta. "She thrives on drama."

The next door was Emma Ray and Lisa Ann's room.

Emma had been protesting a lot lately about having to share a room with Lisa. She was seventeen and Lisa was fourteen. In high school, those three years could make a big difference in maturity, and Emma complained she needed space. Michele and I had shared a room early on until Taylor and Tyler had moved out, and since we were both in our twenties now, Mom and Dad had pumped the brakes on Emma's dream of privacy. I felt for her though. I mean, Michele was only two years younger than me, and sharing a room had been a real pain.

I knocked outside Emma's door. She was at her desk studying some kind of math I'd never been smart enough to take in high school. "Hey, Emma. Mom says dinner in fifteen. This is Etta. She's eating with us tonight."

Emma waved but didn't look up as she quickly punched buttons on a calculator.

"She's really smart," I said to Etta.

Etta laughed. "I can see that."

We had one bathroom upstairs, and two downstairs, the master bath in my parent's bedroom and the guest bath. With eleven people in the house, three bathrooms had never been enough, but we always managed to get to school mostly clean by getting in the shower when we could. Lisa walked up the hall, her willowy body wrapped in a towel.

"Hi," she said. "Bathroom's open if you need it. But

between Butch, Thomas, and me, there is no hot water left."

"Noted," I said. "How's your arm?"

She averted her eyes as her hand raised to the newly bandaged wound on her right bicep. "Fine."

"Bobby Davis, huh?"

Lisa shrugged. "He's just a friend."

"Uh huh."

My sister crossed her eyes at me and stuck out her tongue, reminding me just how young she really was.

"Just be careful," I told her. "Oh, and, Lisa, this is Etta Smith."

"Oh, the doc's kid," she blurted out. "You look like him."

"Tact, Lisa. Jeez."

"No, that's okay," Etta said. "We do have the same coloring, though I like to think I got my chest hair from my mother."

Lisa's eyes bugged. I choked back a laugh. I gave Etta an appraising look. "You'll do just fine," I told her.

We skipped the boys room, since they were all downstairs, and the locker room smell was encroaching into the hallway, I figured it was best. I led her to my room last. "This is mine."

Etta grinned. "You sure like pink."

49

"I used to." My phone beeped. I pulled it out of my back pocket.

Are we still on for tonight? the message read.

I tugged my lower lip between my teeth.

"Boyfriend?" Etta asked.

"No," I denied quickly.

Etta raised her hands, her slender fingers callus-free, and her nailbed well-manicured. "You don't have to tell me," she said. "But the look on your face."

"What look?" I shoved my phone, along with my hands, into my pockets.

"You like whoever sent you the text. You flushed, your pupils dilated, and you looked pleased."

"Who are you? Miss Marple?"

"I'm not nearly that old or British. Plus, no way I'm staying a spinster my whole life just so I can solve crimes." She laughed. "My father...uhm, I mean grandfather, well, William. He taught me how to read people from a young age. He was grooming me to take over as leader of our people."

I didn't really understand Lycanthropic dynamics. I'd heard my parents call Doc Smith a "lone wolf" before, but I hadn't understood what that had meant beyond what I could glean from context. "Therianthropes don't have a leader like that."

"Sure, you do. Isn't Babel Trimmel the mayor? That makes him in charge, right?"

"He's the mayor, but only because he was elected. He works for the town. We don't work for him."

"Huh." Etta grunted. "With lycans, we gain strength from a strong leader."

"Physically?"

"Physically, spiritually, and emotionally," she said. "There is something in our genetics that creates a bond between, and I use the words loosely, an alpha and his or her pack. Or in our case, a leader and his followers."

"Is that why your, uhm, William, had been so unhappy about the Doc and Chavvah?"

"Lycans are weakened by marrying outside our species. Or, at least, that's what I've always been told. It's just not done."

"But Doc married a therianthrope, and they even have a baby. From what I've heard, since he married Chav, there have been seven pregnancies in the lycanthropes. The first pregnancies since..."

"Since I was born." She smiled bitterly. "I know the stories." She paused for a moment, her face awash with melancholy before she pulled her shoulders back and made her expression neutral. "My step-mother is half lycanthrope, and she is a spirit talker. I think that makes the difference."

I couldn't help but think of Cal. "Can you all date someone other than a lycanthrope?"

"Sure. We could totally date outside our species. You know, as long as it's just for fun. Until our mates come along."

"Mates?"

"Yep. Therianthropes don't have mates?"

I shook my head. "We have partners and spouses, and sometimes they last, like my parents, and sometimes they don't." Like Luke and me. "But nothing so definitive as a fated mate."

"Lycans are different in that way. I've never felt the calling, but I've been told it's pretty intense when it happens." She blushed. "I'm sorry. I'm just blathering on and on about our differences. I'm sure we have a lot more similarities than differences. After all, we all put our pants on one leg at a time."

"I jump in with both feet."

She stared at me for second, then we both giggled.

"Time for dinner!" Mom yelled.

I had a million more questions to ask Etta about lycans, but I had a feeling I would hate most of the answers. And I was hyperaware of the unanswered text in my pocket as we headed downstairs to the dining room. Why was Cal pursuing me? Flirting with me? Was it just for fun? Was I an amusement for him until he was struck by the mating lightning bolt? I stopped just short of the dining room and grabbed my phone.

No, I texted back, my heart diving so low in my chest I could feel my belly pulse.

Mom smiled at me as she beckoned. "Come on, baby. Food's getting cold."

CHAPTER FIVE

*T*he clomp of footsteps out in the hall, the boys laughing, annoyed me as I stared at my phone. Cal hadn't texted me since I'd replied. Good. I was much better off staying away from him, especially now that I knew about the whole mating thing that happened in wolves. I wouldn't be anyone's Mrs. In-between. I was glad he hadn't texted me back.

Oh, who was I kidding? Certainly, not myself. It killed me that Cal just let me say no without some push back. I jumped up from my bed and grabbed my purse. I needed to be around someone who loved me but didn't need me. I needed my big brother.

"Mom!" I yelled as I bounded down the stairs. "I'm going over to Taylor's."

"Give him loves from me," she hollered back.

"Done!"

Taylor lived in a residential neighborhood with his boyfriend Eldin Farraday, a fox shifter who worked at the sheriff's department as a deputy with our brother Tyler. Lots of people knew about their relationship. Most of them didn't care, the majority of the ones that did, respected my parents enough to keep their opinions to themselves. Still, there were the few hardcore bigots who couldn't resist a jab at Taylor and Eldin when they were out together.

Music played softly in the house, and the lights were dim. Damn it. Was it Eldin's night off? Suddenly, the music stopped, and the lights went full bright. Cripes. I'd been really quiet.

I knocked, so they wouldn't think I was a burglar. Tayler, tall, buff-blond hair, and lanky like our father, answered the door. His eyes widened in surprise. "Dakota? What are you doing here?"

"I wanted to see my brother, is all. I hope I'm not interrupting," I craned my neck to look behind him, "anything important."

"Two minutes earlier, you would have been," he sighed. "Come in. Eldin got called into work. He's getting dressed now."

"Why in the world would the sheriff call him in on his night off? Have the rabbits stormed the streets?"

He laughed. "Just the Thompsons."

It was a joke between us, because rabbits stereotypically

have a lot of children, but my mom and dad had them beat with us nine.

Eldin came out of the back bedroom. He was thin, shorter than Tyler, and he had a narrow, handsome face. Willy Boden once remarked that he reminded her of a young Tom Hiddleston, and I could definitely see it in his sharp features.

"Dakota." He buckled his utility belt before dipping down to kiss my cheek. "What a nice surprise." I walked into the living room as Eldin opened a safe and took out his weapon. He holstered it. "Too bad I got to run."

"Was there an accident? Please tell me no one died."

"Not yet," he said. "But maybe if I don't get my ass out to Jo Jo Cormans' place."

"Jo Jo?" Michele sometimes went out with Jo Jo, and she'd left the house before me tonight. "What happened at his house? Michele might be out there."

Taylor stopped Eldin before he reached the door. "Can you tell us anything? If Michele is involved, we'd like to know."

"I don't have all the details, but I will tell you, so you don't worry, this is more about the lycans than Jo Jo. Some of the young men from town decided it would be a good idea to go out to the Cormans and harass the lycan-thropes they're hosting. A couple, Dale and Joanna Rivers."

"What about Cal?" I blurted.

My brother and Eldin both gave me a curious look.

"Never mind." I waved off the unasked question. "Did they say who the young men from town are?"

Eldin frowned. "Luke Dwyer and some of his buddies."

"Son-of-a-" If it were possible, I think steam would have poured from my ears. "I'm going with you."

"No, you're not," Eldin said.

"Fine. I'll see you at Jo Jo's then." I hugged my purse close to my body, rummaging for the keys to my truck.

"You can't go," Eldin protested. "This is a police matter, and you're going to get me in trouble with the sheriff if you show up because I talk too damned much."

"I'll just say I was invited."

"By who?" he asked.

I opened my phone and produced the text messages from Cal. "Luke is on the war path about the lycanthropes, and I'm pretty sure it's my fault."

ELDIN MADE Taylor and I sit in the back of his SUV cruiser, and I closed my eyes as the rotating lights bathed the road in a myriad of reds and blues. Taylor stared at me like I'd grown three noses.

"Stop it," I told him. Not even deep breathing exercises could calm the off-the-chart-anxiety threatening to overwhelm me.

"I didn't think you had it in you," Taylor said.

"I don't have anything in me," I childishly replied.

"But you'd like to."

I narrowed my gaze on him. "You're not funny."

"I'm kind of funny."

"Nope," I disagreed.

"Eldin thinks I'm funny."

From the front seat, Eldin said, "It's true. I think Taylor is hilarious."

Taylor gave me a crooked smile. "See. Told you."

My annoyance overtook my anxiety. "You saw my last text. I told him, no. I told him I wouldn't meet him."

"You should have said, yes," Taylor said.

"So, I can get my heart broken. No, thank you. Do you know that lycanthropes have actual mates? They develop like a real bond with the person they are meant to be with."

"Okay," my brother said. "I still don't understand the problem?"

"It can't work between us! The bond only works with another lycanthrope."

Taylor chuckled. "Dakota, sometimes people are meant to be together, even if, on paper, they don't look like they should work."

Eldin reached his hand back and Taylor took it. Eldin drew Taylor's fingers to his lips and gave his knuckles a kiss before letting go and putting both hands back on the wheel.

Taylor's lopsided smile at his boyfriend made me happy and jealous.

"You guys are different."

"Are we?" Taylor asked. "For all intents and purposes, I should have said, no, when Eldin asked me out during Sunny's rehearsal dinner. I knew nothing could come of it, that there was no way to make it work between us. I was really scared how Tyler would react, but here we are four years later. Happy. Even if it all ended tomorrow, I regret not one minute of saying, yes."

"You make it sound so easy."

Eldin let out a barking laugh. "Then he isn't telling the story right."

"Don't be sharing our war stories, now," Taylor cautioned. He winked at me. "We'll save some of our more colorful memories for another time." He pointed toward the windshield. "Corman place just up ahead."

"There were two trucks and a car parked on the road outside Jo Jo's driveway. His dad had built a house for Willy as a wedding present and had given Jo Jo the three-bedroom house when he and Willy had moved out. The black truck at the front belonged to Luke.

"Shoot, shoot," I muttered. My anxiety ratcheting up into high gear. "What is he playing at."

"Maybe this doesn't have anything to do with you," Eldin said as he pulled in behind two other Sheriff's SUVs sitting in the driveway.

"If only that were true. I can't believe Luke is doing this." I peered out my window and watched our brother Tyler talking with Luke, while Willy Boden, another deputy and my mom's best friend, talked to Cal and Dale. The brothers towered over Willy. "He's determined to have the wolves removed from Peculiar."

"Luke?"

"Yes."

Luke's friends included Veronica "Ronnie" Talbert, Jackson Smart, Ludlow Davis, Madison West, Eric Johnson, Delbert Johnson's middle son, and a few others. He must have pulled people from Jackson's party to create this mob. Deputy John Connelly had corralled the group away from the others. The sheriff was talking to Jo Jo, who looked fairly bewildered. Kyle Avery stood behind Jo Jo, and he glared in Luke's direction. When had Kyle become a friend to the wolves?

"This is so not good," I said.

"Stay in the vehicle," Eldin directed.

I reached for the door handle, but Taylor stopped me. "Don't get him in trouble," he told me. "The deputies seem like they got things in hand. I don't see Michele, and nobody looks bloody. We'll just be in the way, and you popping out to come to Cal's rescue might just make things worse for the wolves."

"What makes you think I would jump to Cal's rescue?"

Taylor thinned his lips and shook his head.

"Fine, I probably would," I told him, "but only because Cal has done nothing wrong." Except show up in the nonpredator area on a full moon. Oops. I'd forgotten to mention that to Taylor and Eldin.

"What is it?" Taylor asked.

"Cal ran in the Hackenstraw woods last night."

"How?"

"I don't know. He just showed up."

"You remember him being there? On a full moon?"

"No." But I'd carried the scent of him on me, fur and earthy musk. "But we woke up together in my spot."

"Wow." Taylor stared at me, again, as if my three noses had been joined by a second set of eyes. "Who are you, and what have you done with my sister?"

"Shut up." I wrung my hands as the deputies continued to interview the involved parties. "I can't take this." I needed to get out of the car. I needed to talk to Cal. This was all my fault. I'd drawn attention to him by flirting back, by breaking up with Luke, by trying to reach for something that was beyond me. Maybe if I assured Luke that I wasn't interested in Cal, then he would quit this moronic vendetta. "Maybe I can reason with Luke?"

At that moment, Luke shouted something. Cal surged toward him, and Eldin and Dale helped Willy hold him back. Unfortunately, Luke got away from Tyler, and with Cal's arms restrained, he couldn't defend the fist-blow that landed across his jaw. I cried out and grabbed the door handle before Taylor could stop me.

I raced to the fighting group as Connelly and Sheriff Taylor joined the foray of rushing men, fighting to keep the two men from tearing each other apart. But Cal had broken away from Eldin and Dale, and he'd blocked a second punch from Luke, then took him down in a quick, impressive demonstration of self-defense. Luke's embarrassment as Cal easily held him in place until Connelly and the sheriff could take over, told me that this fight between the two men was far from finished. When Luked tried to yank away, Sheriff Taylor bellowed, "Don't make me put you in handcuffs!" Then he gazed back and forth at Cal and Luke, both coiled for another match. "Walk away! Both of you!"

Instead of going to talk to Luke, as I'd planned, I ran to

Cal. When he saw me, his rage dissolved from his face. I held out my hand. He took it.

I blocked out everyone around us. Anything to keep his eyes locked on mine. "Yes," I told him. "Yes. I'll run with you, but only if we go now."

Cal blinked, the distended veins in his neck flattening as some of the tension uncoiled from him. He nodded. "Let's go."

And so, we ran.

CHAPTER SIX

*T*he Corman's woods were only about a hundred feet behind the house. Cal held my hand, dragging me along with him until we hit the tree line. He stripped his t-shirt over his head when we stopped, and my mouth dropped open in pure yummy awe.

The corner of his mouth tugged into a pleased smile. "Are you planning to wear your clothes when you shift?"

I wasn't normally shy about nudity, but Cal Rivers made my body react in ways that made me self-conscious. I looked back to the Corman house. "You know, Luke and his buddies are probably gone now. We can go back."

Cal pulled his t-shirt through a belt loop in his jeans and walked over. He touched my cheek with the back of his fingers and stared down at me, his eyes reflecting the moon through the trees. "Why are you afraid?"

His question surprised me. "I'm not."

He dropped his hand to his side. "Then what's the problem?"

"We're too different from one another." I couldn't meet his gaze as I said the next part. "Some people just shouldn't be together." Like wolves and deers.

"I like you, Dakota. The first time I saw you, that morning before the Smith wedding, I thought you were the prettiest woman I'd ever laid eyes on. I think you like me, too. Or do I have that wrong? If I do, tell me, and I'll leave you be."

"I like you, too," I said. Gah! Why? I should have lied and lied hard. It would've had been easier to tell him he was wrong. It would have ended this flirtation between Cal and me, and all the problems that came with it. I could've gone back to my quiet uneventful life where men fought over women like my sister Michele and not women like me. "But--"

Cal smiled. "I'll take it." He reached and unbuttoned the top button on his jeans. "Why don't we run tonight, and whatever happens, happens?"

I chuckled when I saw his superhero boxer briefs. "Are you planning on leaping tall buildings in a single bound?"

He grinned. "If it means I get to be close to you."

"And are you faster than a speeding bullet?"

He touched a round scar on his shoulder. "Not usually."

When I frowned, he added, "You should see the other guy."

I felt a mixture of wariness and curiosity. "You've been shot before."

"On the job," he said. He shook his head. "Four years in the army, two spent on tour in the Middle East, I never once took a hit. But less than a year with the highway patrol, and I was shot by a guy who I'd pulled over for going seventy-eight in a sixty-five."

"You were a police officer?" And he was in the military, as well. I touched his scar. "Dangerous work."

"Yes," he said. "Your brother's a deputy, right?"

"Yeah, but we're a small town. He knows almost everyone in the area, and therians know there is a different set of rules for us when it comes to violent acts."

"Like tonight? Luke didn't seem worried in the least about bringing a small mob to come after me."

"I'm sorry about him. He's harmless, honest." I slid my hand absently down Cal's arm, his biceps as big around as my head. I smiled as I thought about the Red Ridinghood story my mother used to read to me.

"What?" Cal asked.

"My, my, what big arms you have."

"The better to hold you with, my dear," Cal said without missing a beat. He slid his arm around my waist and held me close. The hair on his chest tickled my chin as I craned my neck back to look up at him. With his free hand, he caressed my cheek.

"I feel like you've used that line a time or two." I tried not to dwell on the fact that the superhero bulge was pressed against my stomach.

He chuckled, and desire wound through me.

"Maybe," he said. "Is it working?"

"Maybe," I replied. I pressed my palm against his chest. The intense heat of his skin traveled up my arm and filled me with warmth.

"I've never met anyone quite like you, Dakota."

"I find that hard to believe."

"It's true."

"You don't even know me," I told him. I wasn't oblivious enough to think I wasn't pretty. After all, I am my mother's daughter, and deer shifters tended toward a delicate beauty not seen in other therians, but there was nothing else special about me. I wasn't smart like Emma Ray or wild like Michele. Hell, even my youngest sister Lisa was braver than me. "I'm ordinary."

"I can see you believe that," Cal said.

"Because it's true." I leaned my forehead against his chest. "I'm a safe choice."

"A guy just tried to kick my ass because of you. Hardly

seems safe to me." He stroked my hair. "Now, you're either going to have to take off your clothes, or I'm going to have to put mine back on." When I gave him a startled look, he added, "My wolf can't wait to run with your deer."

"Because he likes to chase prey?"

"Because he, we, like leggy blondes." He let me go and stepped back. Immediately, I missed being in his arms. "Are you going to change your mind again?"

"Nope." I unbuttoned my blouse. Cal's gaze made me flush. "But maybe you could turn around until I'm done."

He laughed. "Spoil sport." He turned away, and I quickly stripped down, tucking my phone into my folded jeans, then taking my bra and panties off last.

I breathed in the woods, concentrating on the few whistling birds and chittering squirrels I could hear. I didn't change much outside the full moon, not like my little brother, so it took me a second to latch on to my other nature, but then...ripples of pleasure poured over my skin as my body was remade, my hearing and sense of smell heightened so incredibly that Cal's heartbeat and his delicious musk drowned out any competition for my attention. I flicked my ears back and forth as I tested my split hooves on the hard ground. I barely felt any of the impact thanks to the pads beneath my two toes that acted as shock absorbers. My tail swished as Cal, still with his back to me, dropped his briefs to the ground. Criminently, he really did have a delicious booty.

Playfully, I trotted up behind him and gave his rear and nudge. He stumbled forward, then sharply pivoted to face me. His expression lost all humor as he placed his hand on my head between my ears before the magic of his wolf blurred his features, his thick fur sprouting over his skin until he was standing on four legs, nose to nose with me. The wolf rubbed his large body and his face against my legs, my torso, and finally my neck.

I twitched my ears back and forth in a question that I couldn't ask aloud in my current state. Cal's tongue lolled out of his mouth, and I now understood what the term "wolfish grin" meant. I sniffed the air around me, and it was saturated with the wolf's scent.

He'd put it all over me. He could've have been claiming me as a possession, but I didn't think so. I think he'd done it to protect me. If I smelled like wolf, the other predators would leave me alone. Cal's fur was white around his face, and dark gray, almost black around his ears and neck. The rest of him was gradated shades of gray, white, and black. I'd been around shifted coyotes, and they weren't nearly as big. The sheer size of Cal's wolf made me tremble. I tempered my deer instincts to run away from the big, bad wolf. Instead, I waited for him to take the lead.

Cal barked once as he faced the woods then howled, the melodic sound singing through my bones. After one last look over his shoulder at me, he took off in a trot into the canopy of trees. I released a happy high-pitched bleat I'd been holding onto and leaped in his direction then took off running after him.

Elation overcame me as we loped, unfettered by too much thought. My heart soared when he climbed up onto a fallen log and I jumped nearly eight feet to sail over his head to the other side. I snorted hard at the surprised look on his furry face when I landed, because it was as close to laughing as I could get as a deer. He barked and yipped as he climbed down and ran at me. I didn't have time to drop down, so I could only watch as he launched himself into the air and reciprocated the fly-by. He kept on running when he hit the ground with smooth ease, and I was right behind him, surprised at how well my deer kept up with his wolf. And then, I passed him. I swished my tail as I gained ground, daring him to come after me.

He didn't let me down, his howls and chirps, trailing behind me as he poured on more speed. I don't know how long we were running, but eventually we made our way to the pond near the edge of Brady Corman's property where he'd built the new house. I trotted down for a drink, and Cal joined me at the edge. I knelt on my front knees then back, panting to cool myself in between sips. It was a little muddy, but my animal self didn't mind.

Cal dropped down to his belly beside me and lay his head across my back, and I felt so much contentment in just that little bit of familiarity between us. I'd run with a wolf. We drank together. We lay together. Maybe, just maybe.

A sharp sting in my hindquarter brought my head up sharp. My vision blurred as I looked around. All I could smell was Cal's fur as my soul seemed to separate from my body. I felt disconnected, my movement suddenly sluggish. Then, there was growling, a harsh yip, and my head grew heavy, my thoughts turned cloudy. I tried to shift, but I couldn't concentrate. I heard a noise like a growl, but not quite. I knew I should recognize the sound, but I couldn't make my brain work. Then someone spoke, their words hollow and soft like a distant echo.

"This will all be over soon," it said.

WET DROPS SPLATTERED my naked skin as I blinked daylight from my eyes. I felt like I'd had a V-8 engine dropped on my head during the night. What in the world had happened? The last thing I remembered well was changing into a deer and Cal... I sat up, instantly regretting the speed I'd used, and looked around.

My hand went to my mouth as I stared at the bloody figure of a man, only a few feet away. He wasn't big enough to be Cal, and he had clothes on, so who? Nausea brought the sour taste of bile to my throat as I crawled toward the body. Maybe he was alive. I didn't think so, but I had to check.

When I got a good look at the face, even ripped and covered in blood, I knew without a doubt who it was.

"Luke," I said. "Oh, God. No." I could detect the strong odor of Cal's scent on the body. *No, no, no.* Horror filled me.

Where was Cal? Had he done this? Had Luke found us? Somehow knocked me out, and then fought with Cal? "Please, no," I prayed. "Cal?"

When he didn't answer back, panic took hold of me. What if Cal was dead as well? Had Luke killed him, only to drag me here—I looked around—where ever the hell here was, before dying of his own wounds? I looked around again, the fog beginning to lift. This was the Hackenstraw woods. How in the world had I gotten so far from the Corman property? And where was Cal?

"Cal," I said again. Then as the panic clawed at my guts, I shouted, "Cal!" I scrambled to my feet, but my legs were wobbly, and I found it hard to gain my balance.

"Cal!"

"Dakota!" he bellowed in the distance. "I'm coming!" When he was close enough that I could see him, I stumbled toward him, collapsing into his arms.

"What happened?" I asked, my grief choking my voice.

"It's okay, now," he said. "It's okay."

"It's not," I told him. "Luke's dead. It's not okay." This would be the straw that broke the camel's back for Peculiar, and Luke, who had wanted the lycanthropes gone, would soon get his wish. But at such a high price. I glanced at my dead ex-boyfriend and shuddered. "It's not okay."

CHAPTER SEVEN

*O*nly for the briefest of seconds, did I fantasize about hiding Luke's body. The guilt and shame had lasted much longer. Cal had been much more decisive. Neither of us had our phones, which were in our clothing piles back at the Corman's.

"I'll stay with Luke. You run to town to get the sheriff," he said.

I shook my head. "I don't think that's a good idea. I should stay with Luke."

"Why?"

"They are going to think you did this."

"Do you think I did this?"

"I don't know." I sucked in a breath. "I can smell you on him."

Cal leaned in close to Luke and sniffed. "I see." He shook his head. "That could be from our altercation earlier."

I hated to admit that his reminder eased some of my dread. He'd taken Luke down at Jo Jo's, plus, Luke had punched him. That could explain the scent if it came up in the investigation. Still, would it be enough to keep Cal out of hot water? And would it be enough to keep the lycans from getting kicked out of Peculiar. "Good," I said. "Yes, you both were in physical contact last night."

"I didn't kill Luke," he said.

I felt the blood drain from my face. Luke. Dead. This was someone I knew. Someone I once cared about. The worst part was that my first thought had not been for Luke, it had been to protect Cal.

"You believe me, don't you?"

I nodded. This was a man who spent his adult life protecting and serving, first in the military then as a police officer. But those callings also leant themselves to violence. Still, I believed him. "What happened to us? Do you remember anything?"

"Not much. You made a noise and your fear scent kicked in. I tried to react to defend us but someone shot me with a tranquilizer. It had to be a pretty heavy dose because I was out in seconds."

"I remember feeling a sting in my hind quarters, then everything got pretty fuddled."

"Someone drugged us," Cal said. "And we need to get this reported quickly and get our blood tested right away so we can prove it. You can't be charged with murder if the evidence shows you were incapacitated at the time. Depending on the drug, though, it might be out of our system by now." He put his hands on my shoulders. "So you should go into town. I think the news about Luke will be better coming from you. You're the cooler head between us, and we can't just leave him out here alone."

"You think whoever did this might come back?"

"Or a wild animal scrounging for a meal," Cal replied. "Either way, we can't leave the scene unattended." He forced a smile. "Go. I'll be fine, and I won't touch anything. Promise."

The body buzzed. I knelt down next to Luke.

Cal said, "We shouldn't touch anything."

I used two fingers and plucked Luke's phone from his pocket. A morning alarm was going off on his phone, causing the vibration.

"Now, neither of us have to go." I slid my finger across the front and a lock screen came up. "Shoot."

"What's wrong?"

"It is password protected."

"Use the emergency call feature."

"Right." I slid my finger across the screen and hit the

emergency call button at the bottom of the number screen and waited.

"Peculiar Sheriff's Department. What's your emergency?" a man asked.

"There's been a..." I glanced at Cal. He shrugged. "An accident," I said.

"Do you need an ambulance?" the operator asked.

"No." I shook my head even though he couldn't see me. My voice quavered as I continued, "It's too late for that. Luke Dwyer is dead."

"Dakota?" the operator asked.

Now that he said my name, I recognized Eldin's voice. "Yes."

"Tell me what's happened, and don't leave anything out."

———

AN HOUR LATER, the sheriff arrived with John Connelly and Willy Boden. Sheriff Taylor looked as if he hadn't slept in several days, but dark rings around the eyes was typical for raccoon shifters. Willy had her hand on her weapon as she neared our position.

"Why don't you come over here by me, Dakota." Her voice was strained as she kept a wary eye on Cal.

I glanced at Cal. He nodded.

"Go on," he told me. "I'll be fine."

John Connelly stayed back at the SUV with the radio in his hand while the sheriff walked over the body.

He bent over to get a closer look but didn't touch Luke. He circled his finger around Luke's face. "What happened here?"

"We don't know," I said. "He was like that when I woke up."

"And you?" Sheriff Taylor nodded at Cal.

"It's like Dakota says. I woke up a ways off from here, but when I found Dakota, Dwyer was mangled like that."

"Did you do it?" The sheriff asked.

"No, sir," Cal said.

"What are you all doing here on Hackenstraw's property?"

"I'm pretty sure we were drugged, Sheriff Taylor," I answered. "Neither of us remember leaving the Corman woods."

"Uh huh," he said.

"Test our blood," Cal said. "If we're telling the truth the evidence will be there."

I grimaced, wishing he hadn't told me that some drugs might be out of our system by now and prayed that whatever we'd been hit with wasn't one of them.

Sheriff Taylor looked back to his truck and yelled, "Call

Doctor Smith and Mark Smart." Doc acted as a medical examiner for the town, and Mark Smart was the elected coroner. "We're going to need them both. And tell the doc to bring his vampire kit. He's going to need to take blood samples. Two sets." He stared at Luke's body. "Make that three."

"Does it look like an accident?" Connelly asked.

Sheriff Taylor gave a slight head shake.

Willy, who must have decided Cal wasn't an immediate threat, moved in. "Does your mom know where you're at?" she asked me. Willy was my mom's best friend, so it had surprised me she'd waited so long to ask.

I shivered, goosebumps raising on my skin, as a misting of rain started up again.

"Come on, girly," she said. "I'll get you and the wolfman some blankets from the back then we'll call your Mom. She's probably worried sick about you." She snapped her fingers at Cal as we walked to the back of the SUV. "And you should know better. What happened to keeping your head down until after your probation period is over. It's going to be a hard sell to the town council and the Tri-State Council that keeping you all around is a good idea. Especially, after this."

"I didn't kill him," Cal said.

"It doesn't matter. Small towns operate on appearance." She gestured with a wave of her hand. "This is non-predator territory, and you shouldn't be here. Like, at all.

This is not going to go over well with the folks in town who are already afraid."

"I didn't kill him," Cal said again.

"You were fighting with him just last evening." Willy threw up her hands. "Then you took off into the woods with his girlfriend."

"He tried to fight me. I didn't fight with him," Cal said.

"And ex-girlfriend," I added. "I broke it off with Luke a while back. He just couldn't take no for an answer."

"And that's why you killed him," Willy said.

"No!" Cal and I both said simultaneously.

"I believe you, kid. Honest," Willy said, "but it's not how other people will see it. This looks like a clear case of love triangle gone wrong."

"Cal and I aren't even dating," I protested.

Willy pursed her lips and narrowed her gaze on me as Cal wrapped a blanket from the back around my shoulders.

"You want to stick with that story?" she asked.

"I've asked Dakota out," Cal said. "But we haven't gone on an actual date."

Willy put her hand on her hips. "And what do you call last night?"

"An impulsive decision," I said. One, that up until we were drugged and had awakened next to a dead body, I hadn't regretted. "Can we not tell my mom? I mean, isn't there such a thing as confidentiality with police stuff?"

"Nope," Willy said. "No such thing. Besides, do you really want your mom finding out from someone else, like..." She gestured toward Connelly. "You know he's going to tell his wife, and if Selena knows, everyone knows."

I groaned. "That's true. I suppose it's better if it comes from me."

Doctor Smith showed up next. He got out and walked around to the passenger side and opened the door for is wife Chavvah. She slid out of her seat, her large belly leading the way.

A green truck roared in a few seconds later, and I groaned again. It was my brother Tyler, only not on official business. My brother wore jeans and a red and black flannel shirt. He slid his truck to a halt, tearing up the grass in the process. He jumped out of the truck, his finger pointing at Cal, as he shouted, "Stay away from her, you freak."

I was too dumbstruck to do more than step into his charging path.

"Get out of the way, Kota."

"No," I told him. "Not until you settle down."

"That... that..." he sputtered. "He killed Luke!"

"He did not!" I balled my hands into fists. "How did you even hear about this?" I glared at Willy. She shook her head. We both turned to Connelly, and he quickly averted his gaze.

"It doesn't matter who told me. The point is, you don't know anything about this guy. You've known Luke your whole life. Why are you taking his side?"

"Because he's a decent man, Tyler. And not a hot head like you."

My brother jerked his chin as if I'd landed a physical blow. "I am worried about you," he said through clenched teeth.

"Worry less and listen more."

His tone deepened as his annoyance rose. "I don't trust him."

"Him or his kind?" I asked. When he didn't answer me, I said, "Dude, you've got to stop drinking the fruit punch. The lycanthropes aren't the ones who are starting trouble. They didn't round up a mob to go to Luke's house last night, did they? No. That was a therianthrope."

"One who's dead now," Tyler said. "Or does his impulsive act last night warrant an execution."

Chavvah Smith came to stand next to me. "I'm curious, Tyler Thompson. Do you just have a problem with Cal? Or do you have a problem with all my wolves?" Her voice held a dangerous edge that made me want to take three steps back.

"I..." he lowered his eyes. "I don't have any problem. I'm just worried about my sister."

"Willy and I have her," Chavvah said. "You can go."

"And don't tell your mother," Willy warned him in a tone that brokered no argument. "This is something she should hear from your sister, not you."

Tyler glared at me, but he knew when he was outnumbered. "Fine. But if you don't tell Mom immediately--"

"I will." I felt like a petulant child, but unlike Taylor, Tyler brought out the worst in me. For identical twins, they couldn't have been more opposite in personalities.

After Tyler left, I hovered with Cal on the other side of the vehicles while the investigators investigated. "Don't take my brother too seriously," I told him. "It takes him a while to warm up to strangers."

Cal pulled my blankets tighter around my shoulders. "And what about you? How long does it take you to warm up to strangers?"

"Come on, you two," Chavvah said. "Sheriff Taylor says I can take you both home after Doc draws your blood."

"Great," I said with zero enthusiasm.

"I should go with Dakota. I can try and explain to her parents--"

Willy and Chavvah both said, "No," at the same time.

Chavvah said, "Look, Cal. I know this isn't your fault. But the wolves are on loose footing around here, and you heading into Peculiar right now is a bit like walking on limestone. Take the wrong step and it will crumble beneath you. I have too much to lose if the good folk around here decide you all have to leave." She put her hand on her round belly and gazed at Cal. "We all do."

"I get it," he said. "I'll go back to Jo Jo's and lay low today."

Chav gave him a tight-lipped smile. "Good. It's settled then. I'll drop you off first, so, Ruth doesn't have to see me pull up to the house with both of you."

"I'm sorry," I said to Cal. He put his arms around me, and I didn't pull away. This might be the last time he ever held me. I couldn't deny myself the moment. "This is all my fault."

"We'll get it figured out, Dakota. Someone or something killed Dwyer. The police will figure out who, and we'll put this tragedy behind us."

If only, I thought, as I breathed in his scent. If only.

CHAPTER EIGHT

"*I* swear to heaven, child, if you were younger, I'd ground you into old age," my mother said. "What were you thinking taking off with that man? You don't know anything about him."

"Neither do you," I snapped back, surprising both of us. It was six-twenty in the morning, and my thoughts still felt a bit fuddled and heavy. I rubbed my inner arm absently where Doc Smith had drawn blood before we'd left the scene. Willy had taken our preliminary statement, but we were told to come down to the station sometime this afternoon to fill out official witness statements. I hoped the Doc would find something to prove we were drugged before then.

My mom shook her head. "I'd expect something like this from Michele but not you." She paced back in forth in the kitchen. "When your father hears about this, he's going to have a fit."

I'd heard mom say those same words to Michele before, and to my knowledge, Dad hadn't had a single fit, yet. "None of this was meant to upset you mom. It just happened." Just usually not to me. I sighed. "I don't know why anyone would want to harm Luke. I only know for sure that Cal didn't do it."

"And how do you know that?" she asked. "According to you, you were drugged and can't remember a dang thing."

The only proof I had that Cal didn't do it was my intuition and instinct, neither of those would hold up in court. How could I explain it to Mom without sounding like a silly, love-sick girl, and not a rational woman who draws reasoned conclusions? I couldn't, so I didn't try. "I just know."

"That's the kind of evidence that clears murder cases all the time," she said sarcastically. I'd heard her take this tone with some of my siblings, but never with me. I found I didn't care much to be on the wrong foot of Mom's ire.

"They haven't said it was murder." Not yet, anyhow. I was sure it would come. We didn't end up drugged and set up to look guilty because Luke had been accidentally killed. No. Someone had wanted to frame Cal. But who? As far as I knew, Luke had no enemies.

Mom echoed my thoughts. "Why in the world would someone want to kill Luke? He was a respectable boy from a good family. This has to be about the wolves."

"Maybe," I said. I couldn't get Luke's threat to report Cal

to the town council off my mind. It was damning as a motive. Even if Cal hadn't harmed Luke, he might have told one of the other werewolves. But would someone kill to prevent being kicked out of a town? It seemed like a stretch, but who knew. I'd watched true crime shows where people had been killed for less.

"Tell me what you're thinking," Mom said. "And don't hold anything back."

"Cal was with me when I woke up yesterday on the Hackenstraw property. Luke saw him and threatened to tell. Maybe Cal told one of the other lycanthropes. Maybe they decided to stop Luke before he could," I admitted as a possibility. "Luke didn't show up at your meeting, though, did he? You would have said something about it before dinner last night, right?"

A tremor started in my hands and went to my knees as my vision became spotty. "I don't feel so good." I braced myself against the table to keep myself upright as the full weight of my circumstances wore me down. Luke was dead, and it was possibly my fault. Dear, God, I hoped that wasn't true.

Mom pulled out a chair for me at the table. "Sit down, dear." Her tone was civil again. "You must be in shock, seeing that boy like that."

My shoulders began to shudder as a sob caught in my throat. "It was awful." I rubbed my upper arms, taking comfort from the memory of Cal's embrace. "I've never seen anything like it."

"Poor thing," Mom said. "You're pale as a ghost. You were handling it all so well, I didn't even think about the toll it might be taking on you."

"I don't understand how this happened. Luke didn't have enemies."

"Yes, he did," Michele said. Mom and I both startled as my younger sister walked into the kitchen. Her dark blond hair was loose around her shoulders, and she wore a low-cut blouse with tight jeans.

"What do you mean?" I asked. "Who hated Luke?"

"I can't say," Michele said. "I shouldn't have said anything." She grabbed a Granny Smith apple from a bowl on the counter. "It's just...Luke wasn't a good guy."

"You explain yourself, little miss," my mom said.

Michele raised a brow. "Can't," she said. "Gotta go. Sunny expects me at her house in fifteen minutes to watch the kids." She gave mom a smooch on the cheek then cast a sympathetic look in my direction. "I have a feeling this town is going to be reeling soon. I'm glad you dumped his stupid ass when you did." And as quickly as she'd breezed into the conversation, Michele had breezed out.

My mom sat down, her expression bewildered. "Dumped who?"

"Luke," I said.

"I thought you were still seeing him." Ugh. I couldn't take

the look of betrayal she was casting in my direction. "Why didn't you tell me?"

"I haven't been seeing him for a couple months now. You were so happy when I started dating him. I didn't have the heart to tell you that I couldn't like him the way you wanted me to like him. I didn't want to disappoint you."

"Oh, my darling girl." Mom reached across the table and took my hand. "You have never disappointed me." She sighed. "Well, maybe a little last night. Running off, staying out all night, getting yourself drugged. You could have been killed! That's the only reason I'm upset. I don't care who you date. I liked Luke for you because I thought you liked Luke for you. And I was angry about Cal because, you were placed in a very vulnerable position last night while you were out with him."

I didn't try to hold back the tears. Mom reached over the counter and handed me the roll of paper towels. "I want you happy and safe, Dakota. That's all I've ever wanted for any of my children."

I knew she believed what she was saying but as the oldest girl in the family, Mom and Dad both expected more from me than my siblings. I didn't blame them. I'd taken on the role of helper and caretaker without complaint. Sometimes, though, it was hard to live up to the standard I'd created for myself. "I'm going to go lay down for a while, if that's okay. I still don't feel well."

Mom nodded. "That's a good idea. I'll let your dad know you won't be working today."

I passed Lisa Ann in the hall. She was dressed and had her school backpack on. It surprised me because usually she was the last one ready and the last one out the door. I usually had to tell her to get out of bed half a dozen times before she'd actually get up. "Where you off to so early?"

She gave me a funny look then brusquely said, "School," as she brushed past me.

I did not have the capacity to deal with a moody teen this morning, so I didn't even try. "All right, then. You have a nice day."

I TOSSED AND TURNED A LOT, but I definitely did not sleep. My phone was still somewhere in the woods at Jo Jo's. Chav wouldn't let me out of the truck when she dropped off Cal, so I wasn't able to get it back. But not having a phone meant I couldn't check on Cal. His brother and sister-in-law had looked as angry as my mom. He was probably still being grilled by them. The longer I stewed about what had happened, the more Michele's words haunted me. Luke wasn't the good guy we thought he was. What did she mean? Maybe I could sneak away to Sunny's and catch Michele in private. Would she tell me? She seemed adamant she was going to keep her secrets. Even so, I had to try. I'd covered for her more times over the years than I had fingers and toes. She owed me.

All my younger brothers and sisters were at school, and Mom had gone to help Dad in the shop. Still, I waited until after lunch to make my escape. I'd left my truck at Taylor's and I had a hideaway holder inside the driver side front wheel well with an extra key. It was a mile across town to Taylor's place, but I made quick time cutting through yards and between businesses. Sunny's house was a mile or two from Jo Jo's. Maybe I'd swing by after to get my phone, and if I happen to run into a certain werewolf, well, it would be pure coincidence. Hah.

Sunny and Babel Trimmel's house was a darling little one-story cabin just off the road with a covered porch and a two-seater swing. Michele's red car was in the driveway, but so was Sunny's gold van. Shoot. I considered driving past the house without stopping but decided being a coward wouldn't help Cal and the lycanthropes. I needed to know what secret or secrets my sister harbored.

"I won't be here long," I heard Sunny say to Michele as she opened the door. When she saw me, she said, "Come in, Dakota. I've been expecting you."

Ooh-key dokey. "How did you know?"

"I'm a psychic." She pointed to her head. "In case, you've forgotten."

Wow, either her visions which had been unreliable in the past were getting sharper or... I grimaced. "Mom called you, didn't she."

Sunny smiled. "That, too." I walked past her as she waved

me in. Baby Jude, who was now four-years-old ran around the living room making *vroom-vroom* noise as he crashed into the couch, the love seat, and the recliner. Dawn, only a year younger than him, giggled and clapped her hand every time he wrecked.

Michele encouraged the play, while keeping Jude away from anything he could permanently damage, like the television set. She glanced up at me. "I owe Sunny ten dollars."

"I'll take it out of your babysitting fee," Sunny said. She winked at me. "Michele thought you'd show up this morning, but I told her you wouldn't be here until after noon."

"How did you--"

She shrugged her narrow shoulders. "It's the sweet spot between lunch and dinner in order to avoid your parents disapproval."

"That's mean," I said.

Michele snickered. "But true."

"Look, I've known you all for several years now, and it's not hard to read the dynamic of your family. You do all the worrying about your parents which frees the other kids up to worry only about themselves."

"Hey!" Michele said. She scooped Judah up under one arm and Dawn under the other. "I worry plenty about other people."

Sunny's body grew still for a second then she strolled across the room to Michele and lightly touched her face. "You should tell Dakota what you know," she said.

"I can't. I promised."

"And someone's been killed. Some promises can't be kept," she said. She took her children from my sister. "I'll take the babies outside. You talk to your sister."

Michele, her face solemn, nodded. "Okay."

"Wait," I said to Sunny. "Did you have a vision of who killed Luke?" Because that would save us all a heap of trouble.

"No." She shook her head. "Oh, and I had a premonition this morning about you. I'm not sure what it means but I see dancing chickens in your future."

"You're so weird," I told her.

"Hey, I see what I see." On that note, she took the children outside to play.

Michele sat on the couch and patted the cushion next to her. "Come and sit."

I did. "What's going on, Mishy? What did you mean this morning about Luke not being a good guy?"

"Come on," she said. "You had to sense it. You did break up with him after all."

I flushed guiltily. "Not because I thought he was a bad guy."

"Then why?"

I twirled a lock of my hair between my fingers and toed the carpet, embarrassed by my answer.

"Oh," Michele said. "Now you have to tell me. Was he a bad kisser?" She gasped. "Bad in bed? Ooo. No. Don't tell me if you were having sex with that asshole."

"I wasn't having sex with him, and he kissed just fine. Just not fine enough to make me want to have sex with him."

"Then why did you break up with him?"

I met my sister's gaze. "He was boring."

She snorted her surprise. "You're boring. It seems like a match made in Heaven."

Like with Sunny, Michele's words hurt. "I might seem boring on the outside, but on the inside, I'm turbulent as hell."

"All right," she said, raising her hands in surrender. "I'm just surprised is all." Uncharacteristically, she patted my knee in a gesture of comfort. Her voice held a tone I wasn't used to in Michele. Serious and somber. "What I'm about to tell you is going to be hard to hear."

"I'm a big girl," I told her.

She nodded. "Two months ago, Katrina Wells went with me to a party out at Jackson Smart's new place. Sometime during the night, I'd split off from her to hang out with Brad Sader."

"Brad Sader?" Brad was a fox shifter who had left Peculiar after graduation to go to college in the city.

"He was home for a weekend, but let's not get side-tracked," she said. "This isn't about me. Anyhow, I went off with Brad, and I left Karina alone at the party. Luke was there, along with Eric Johnson, Ronnie Talbert, and a few other people we knew. I didn't think--" Michele's eyes glittered with new tears. "I wouldn't have left her." She stared at me, her gaze stark.

"What happened?"

"She...she doesn't remember much. She felt funny and everything else beyond that is a little fuzzy for her, but when she woke up, Luke was on top of her."

I gasped. "No."

"I swear it, Kota. For the longest time, she thought she had hallucinated the whole thing, because she'd passed out and when she woke up, she couldn't remember much else, and Luke acted as if nothing had happened between them."

"How come you didn't tell me sooner? I was dating him for heaven's sake." Could steady, reliable Luke, from a good family, Dwyer really be a rapist?

"I only found out yesterday," Michele said. "And you had already broke things off with him. I swear if you were still seeing Luke, I would have told you. I wouldn't have let you keep going out with him. And Ree Ree made me promise not to tell you or anyone." Her brow furrowed, and her eyes darkened. "She's pregnant. The bastard took advantage of her, and he didn't even bother to use any protection."

"You say she felt fuzzy?" Maybe she'd been drugged in the same way that Cal and I had been drugged. Rage blossomed inside me, and until this moment, I didn't know my capacity to hate was so vast and wide. I had been dating a monster.

"Yes. She said she drank a cup of beer and felt strange and euphoric after."

"Does Kyle know?" He had been shooting daggers with his eyes at Luke the night before. He'd glowered at me at the clinic. Probably because of my connection to Luke.

Michele sighed. "Yes, he knows. He's so angry."

"Angry enough to kill Luke?" Hell, I was angry enough to kill him right now.

Michele's eyes widened. "No. He wouldn't." She stood up. "Would he? I overheard Mom's interrogation this morning. You think someone drugged you. Do you think that's what happened?"

"Maybe," I told her. "I don't know. Doctor Smith is running my blood work to see if there is any trace of some kind of tranquilizer in it. It could be revenge, and Cal and I were used to throw suspicion off the real motives."

"Ree told me that Kyle is standing by her. He wants to raise the baby as his own." She rubbed her hands down her thighs as worry darkened her features. "He wouldn't risk everything for revenge. But... he had shut down Katrina when she'd suggested they go to the police."

"The sheriff needs to know. If nothing else, we should tell Tyler, and he can investigate."

"Tyler and Luke were friends," Michele said. "Do you really think he's going to believe Karina? He puts her in the punk category with Kyle."

I stood up. "We'll make him believe her."

"Wait," Michele said. "Wait until I've had a chance to talk to Karina. She should have the option to talk to the police first."

"Okay." I started toward the door.

"What are you going to do now?" Michele asked.

If I couldn't tell the police about Luke and Karina, I knew someone else who had experience in law enforcement. Maybe between Cal and I, we could start our own investigation. I didn't want my sister to interfere, or worse, tell on me, so I said, "I'm going to find my phone."

CHAPTER NINE

"*H*owdy-do," said Etta Smith when she got out of her car. We'd both pulled into Jo Jo's drive about the same time. "Did Cal call you, too?"

"I don't have my phone," I said dryly. Why had Cal called Etta? "Is there some kind of meeting going on?"

"Apparently, he needs my expertise." She nudged my shoulder as we walked to the front door. "How come you didn't tell me you were interested in Cal last night at dinner? I would not have gone on and on about, you know." She waved her hand elaborately.

"The fact that we can't ever really be together," I said.

Her expression soured. "Yes. That. I mean, it doesn't mean you can't have fun. And Cal is certainly a lot of fun." She wiggled her brows.

"How much fun is he?" I asked tersely.

Etta chuckled. "I've heard," she amended. "I have no personal experience with Cal, er herm," she cleared her throat, "recreationally."

"So, he's never had a...mate?"

She placed a friendly hand on my shoulder. "Girl, he wouldn't be single now if he had found his one."

I heard several voices inside the house. Maybe this was a strictly lycanthrope pow-wow, and as the lone theri-anthrope, I was inserting myself into a situation where I would not be wanted. "I'm not interrupting anything, am I?"

The door opened. "We're trying to break into Luke's phone," Cal said as a way of greeting. "Hey, Dakota. Are you doing all right?"

"How good is your hearing?" I asked, my stomach flip-flopping at the sight of him in steel gray athletic tricot pants and a tight turquoise t-shirt that stretched across his chest in a way that displayed all his yumminess.

He smiled. "Pretty good. Besides, I saw you pull up outside."

"I'm doing okay." He wasn't wearing shoes, which just added to his sex appeal. "Uhm, you?"

"I'll be better once Etta cracks Dwyer's password." He gave the silver-haired beauty a pithy look.

Etta stuck her tongue out at him. "You know cracking a passcode is near impossible, right?"

"I've caught you reselling after market," he used finger quotes around the last two words, "phones. And you've been hacking computers since you were a pup."

Etta rolled her eyes. "First, you don't have to hack and unlocked phone to unlock it for resale, you just need to do a factory reset, but you don't want me to do that."

"I don't?" Cal said as we walked inside Jo Jo's house.

"Nope," Etta said. "Not if you want to look at Dwyer's call logs. A factory reset takes it back to zero. We'll lose any data he might've had on that phone."

"Well, shit-balls," Dale Rivers said as he came out of the kitchen and into the living room. "What can we do then?"

"I could pop the sim card out, do a factory reset, then put it back in. It won't show any texts or call logs, but it will give you any contacts he has saved. I'm not sure what good that will do you, though."

"What about storage?" I asked. "Luke liked to take pictures and videos. Is there any way to get into his gallery? There might be something on there. Some clue as to why someone would want him dead. I have a micro USB card in my phone that I store pictures on and use for games and such, maybe he does as well."

"That's a good idea," Etta said.

"I have one every once in a while." Just not lately, for example, running off in the night with a guy I could never really have.

Jo Jo came out of one of the back rooms. Over the years, he'd transformed from the lanky boy who used to chase Michele and I around school, to a man in his own right. His body had thickened, and become more muscular, but he still had the wiry look of a coyote shifter. The summer after high school he'd spent a couple of months with his mom's folks in Springfield, and he'd come home with tattoos and a dozen or more piercings. That's when he'd become interesting to Michele. She liked to walk the edge when it came to her personal life. Still, I hated how she'd strung him along the past two years. If he was smart, he wouldn't waste his heart on someone who couldn't recip-rocate. The revelation jarred me. Wasn't that exactly what I was doing with Cal? Wasting my heart.

"Dakota," Jo Jo said. "I am so sorry." He crossed the room to me and gave me a hug. "Cal told me about Luke. I can't say I ever liked the guy, but I wouldn't wish him dead."

Luke had always been well respected in the community, and I thought he and Jo Jo were friends, so the statement surprised me. "What did Luke do to make you not like him?"

"Nothing particularly. It was the way he treated people who he thought were beneath him. He didn't show you that side, because he wanted to impress you. But Luke thought of himself as superior to a lot of people. Espe-cially those of us who didn't have the same advantages."

I tried to remember all the times I'd been with Luke. We'd either gone out on our own or, on a few occasions, hung out with his two best friends. Eric Johnson's parents owned the general store and Jackson Smart's parents owned the funeral home. He would have considered them in his class, so I wouldn't have noticed. My parents owned an auto shop, but with eleven mouths to feed, they certainly didn't have money. And I was a regular grease monkey for the love of Pete. "If he was classist, why in the world had he dated me?" I asked.

"Come on, Dakota," Jo Jo said. "Your parents are on the town council, they're friends with the mayor, they have direct connections to the Tri-State Council, your brother is a deputy with aspirations to become sheriff one day, and to top it off, you're a beautiful girl who is nice to a fault."

I crossed my arms over my chest and frowned. "I'm not nice to a fault."

"If you say so," he said. "But I've seen you apologize to a spider for accidentally stepping on it."

"Spiders eat mosquitoes. They are nature's great equalizers."

He chuckled and shook his head. Peripherally, I saw Etta staring at Jo Jo in a way that I recognized. It was the same way I looked at Cal. Apparently, I wasn't the only one who wanted what I couldn't have.

Cal stood beside me. "I have your phone and your clothes. I got them from the woods this morning. They're back in my room."

All eyes seem to be on me as I said, "Lead the way."

"You two kids don't do anything I wouldn't do," Dale Rivers said.

"Then that leaves it wide open," Etta added.

My cheeks warmed as I tried to ignore them. I followed Cal down a narrow hall to the second door on the left. The bedroom had beige walls, a full-size bed with a blue bedspread, unmade, a small dresser that had been painted brown, probably from the used furniture store in town. There was no decor to speak of, reminding me that these lycanthropes had come to Peculiar with not much more than the clothes on their backs in order to escape a tyrant.

I went inside ahead of Cal, and he closed the door behind us. When I turned around, he wrapped me in his arms. I sagged against him, the sound of his heart soothing my worries. "All I've wanted to do today is find you and hold you. If Chavvah hadn't given me strict orders not to go into town, I would have run straight to your house after she dropped me off. Watching her drive away with you was the hardest thing I've done in a while."

He smoothed my hair back and gazed down at my face. "I feel like my whole world is being turned inside out," I said. "What I thought was up is down, and what I thought was right is wrong." I decided to confide in him about Karina Wells. "My sister Michele says Luke took advantage of a girl when she was incapacitated at a party. He probably drugged her to have sex with her."

"To rape her," Cal said.

I nodded. "How could I go out with someone like that and not know it? I thought I was a good judge of character, but I was so far off base with him."

"Did you love him?"

"No," I said. "I never did."

"Then maybe you're a better judge than you think."

"Perhaps." The heat of his skin pressed in on me, and I slid my arms around his waist. "We have to find out who killed Luke. You were a police officer, right?"

"Highway patrol," he said. "It consisted mostly of pulling over speeding cars and assisting with the occasional wreck out on the highway. I didn't do a lot of investigative work."

"We should see if Doc Smith has our blood results in, yet."

"He'll give the sheriff those results when he gets them, but probably not us. They'll save that for when they interrogate us over our witness accounts."

"Interrogate?"

"If they think I'm responsible, they are going to grill us for hours."

"Why?"

"Because if we're lying, a deep dive interrogation might rattle us to say something incriminatory."

"But we're not lying. I've known Sheriff Taylor my whole life. He has no reason to doubt me."

"Not even to protect your lycanthrope lover?"

"We are not lovers!"

Cal gave me a small smile. "Not yet." He winked.

I smacked his chest, but not with any real conviction. "What have I gotten myself into with you?"

"Nothing yet, but I'm hoping we get lots of time to find out."

"Etta," I said.

"Weird segue," Cal said. "But go on."

"Etta works at the Doc's office. She could get a peek at the blood work, and maybe even the autopsy report. But do you think she would? She and her dad aren't on the best terms. This might be too much to ask." I tugged my lower lip between my teeth and Cal's bulge shifted in his pants. I met his gaze as a low, rumbly growl vibrated his chest.

"Sorry," he said. "When you bite your lip like that it does all kinds of things to me."

"For example?" I teased.

"I think you've already felt a demonstration." The bulge had become thick and hard against me. "Do you really need more examples?"

Mate. Mate. Mate, I told myself. *One day, Cal will find a mate, and I will be a distant memory.* I sighed at my inner nag. "Why are you pursuing me?"

"Seriously?" he asked.

"Yes, seriously." We were from two different worlds. "What do you want from me, Cal?"

He cupped my neck, his fingers weaving into my hair. "Everything. All of you. And if that's too much, whatever you're willing to give me."

"Why? Why would you want me when we can't possibly have a future together?"

"I can't predict what's going to happen down the road, Dakota. But when I think about my life, I know it's better if you're in it." He let his hand drop to his side. "But I can take no for an answer. If you don't want to be with me, or at the very least, date me, just say the word. It'll be difficult, but I'll let you go."

"Don't," I told him.

"Don't what?"

I raised my arms and locked my fingers behind his neck as I went up on my tippy-toes. I kissed him. "Don't let me go."

For a second he didn't move, and I had a horrifying thought he might reject me, but then his arms encircled me again, and he pressed his soft lips against mine. He pulled me closer, a rumble thundering in his chest as I opened for him, taking his tongue into my mouth. He picked me up, and I wrapped my legs around his hips as he turned and pressed me up against the wall. I moaned when he thrust his groin against my aching core.

Mercy, I thought, as I gyrated against him, wishing there was a whole lot less fabric between us down there. My breath quickened as he moved the kiss down my jaw to my neck, his hand skimming up my side to caress my breast. I moaned again. I wanted more. So much more. I slid my hand between us and rubbed my palm against his thick, hard, and really large erection. Holy schnizzle. "Jayzus," I whispered. "What a big, dick you have?" Had I just said that out loud?

Cal's chuckle against my skin confirmed that I had. "The better to--"

"Hey, you two aren't alone in the house!" a shout came from the hall. "Wolves and coyotes have really good hearing."

"Shit, shit, shit," Cal said.

I laughed as he set me down on the floor, because it was either that or cry. I grimaced. "Do you think they heard that last part, because that was really out of character for me?"

Cal grinned before kissing me in a way that curled my toes. After he whispered in my ear, "I'll play big, bad wolf to your Red Riding Doe anytime you want."

Oh, the fantasies that played out in my mind. "Let's just

make it through this investigation first, then we'll figure the rest out."

A sharp knock snapped me out of the heady lust-filled haze.

Etta said, "Get decent. You two need to see what I found."

I frowned at Cal. "We are decent."

He raised a brow. "Speak for yourself." He stepped back, and his erection pointed in my direction. "It's going to take me a second, but you go on out. It'll be easier if I'm not looking at you."

I giggled as I opened the door and backed out of the room into the hallway. Etta grabbed my hand and led me down the hall into the kitchen where Dale and Jo Jo looked both livid and disgusted.

The smile I wore faded. "What's wrong?"

"I can't believe it," Jo Jo said. He slammed his fists down on the table next to a laptop. "That bastard."

My insides twisted. "Show me."

"No one should see these," Dale said.

"Show me," I said again. In less than a minute, I regretted those words more than I had anything in my life. There were lewd pictures of Karina Wells on his phone, and she wasn't the only one. I recognized Veronica Talbert as well. There were two more girls that I didn't recognize. Integrators, maybe. All of them had their eyes closed, posed in various positions. My stomach churned, and bile rose in my throat. Had he kept these photos for personal use or had Luke shared these photos with his friends? Either way was heinous. I wanted to go home and take a thousand showers to scrub every place he'd ever made contact with me. The vile inhumanity of how he'd treated these women disgusted me to no end.

I closed the laptop and pushed it away from me and met Cal's gaze. "I would never presume to take justice into my own hands," I said. "But if anyone deserved to die, I'm pretty sure it is Luke Dwyer."

CHAPTER TEN

"*W*e have to take this to the sheriff. It goes a long way to proving there are more people with a motive to kill Luke than Cal," Dale said.

Like me, for an example. I clenched my fists. It sickened me that I had dated someone capable of such despicable acts.

"Dale's right. We can't let this go unreported," Jo Jo said. "People need to know the kind of guy Luke really was, not the kind of guy they thought he was. At this point, whoever killed him should get a medal as far as I'm concerned."

"It feels a little like using his victims. If they were all drugged, they might not even know it happened to them. We could be dredging up things better left undredged," Etta said. "Sometimes you shouldn't shake the tree."

"You can't believe that. Wouldn't you want to know if

110

something like that happened to you, even if you couldn't remember?" I asked.

"No," she said. "I wouldn't."

"I would."

"That's easy to say when you've never had anything bad happen to you." Her eyes flashed with remorse. "That's not fair," she said. "I don't know anything about your past."

My chest squeezed. "And I don't know anything about yours." Had something happened to Etta? Something she'd sooner forget than remember? I met her gaze, a new understanding forming between us. I gave her a solemn nod. "I agree with Etta. We should wait a bit to see what turns up before taking those pictures to the police."

Cal came into the kitchen. He'd changed into a pair of jeans that were just the right amount of snug on his muscular thighs. Jayzus, the man was hot-damn hot. I couldn't believe he didn't set off fire alarms every time he walked into a room. I tugged my lower lip between my teeth, then hastily let it go when I remembered the reaction he'd had when we'd been in the bedroom.

Etta threw me a quick glance and gave me a knowing brow wiggled.

I threw her one back that said, "stop it."

"I heard you guys talking out here," Cal said, glancing meaningfully at the laptop. "I don't need to see the pictures to know they're bad. Are we sure we don't want to take them to the sheriff right now?"

"I'm not sure," Dale said. "I think we should. After all, it could go a long way to throw suspicion somewhere else."

Etta shook her head emphatically and stood up from the table. She began to pace the kitchen floor. "Those girls are going to have enough to deal with when they learn about these pictures, if they don't already know. I won't have us using them because it might take the heat off us. Cal is innocent. We just need to find a way to prove it."

"Being found guilty of murder has a penalty of death in the therianthrope world," Jo Jo said. "You should be doing everything to make sure that doesn't happen."

"It's the same for lycanthropes." Etta tossed her silver hair over her shoulder and cast her defiant gaze at Jo Jo. "But we can't use these women as a means to an end." She gave Dale and Cal a nod. "We can't do that. Not anymore."

I knew from stuff my mom had said that Etta had been raised to lead the wolves, and in this moment, I believed she would have been good at the job. "I'm okay with waiting. Any of those girls could have been my sister, or me, and I'm thankful it wasn't, but if it had been, I do think I'd want to know, but Etta's right, I wouldn't want a bunch of strangers, or even worse, friends and family, ogling those photos. Luke is dead. He can't hurt anyone ever again. So, for now, we should keep this quiet unless we need it." My heart ached for Karina Wells. She was pregnant. Kyle wanted to be the father. Making Luke's deeds public would make her difficult situation even more impossible. "Besides, what if the murder has nothing to do with these girls? If we give this to the police, it's all they'll focus on. I think we should do a little investigating ourselves."

Jo Jo poured himself a cup of tea and sat down. "I'm in."

Dale's nostrils flared. He rubbed his meaty hands over his face. "We should talk to Chavvah and Billy Bob first. What we do will affect them as well as us. And with Joanna pregnant, sticking our noses in this mess feels like a big risk."

"My nose is inches deep in this already, brother," Cal said. "But I understand if you don't want to be involved." Cal put his hand on my shoulder. "If Dakota wants to get the lay of the land before we give our statements, I'm with her."

Etta's eyes flicked in my direction. "Me, too."

Dale made a noncommittal noise then sighed. "Fine, but if things start looking liked they might go sideways, we go to the police immediately."

Cal patted his older brother on the back. "I knew I could count on you."

Dale rubbed the tip of his finger over a scratch in the table surface. "Yeah, yeah."

I clapped my hands. "Great. We don't have a lot of time

before Cal and I have to give our official statements. I know most of the crew Luke hung out with. Talking to his buddies is as good a place to start as anywhere." I turned to Etta. "We'll see what we can find out on our own, and if we or the police don't find any evidence to clear Cal, then we'll go to the sheriff with the pictures. But only as a last resort." I tried to smile reassuringly. "I understand those women are victims, but it doesn't mean one of them didn't do it."

Dale, who still looked skeptical said, "We'll keep this between us for now." He looked at Cal. "I don't want Joanna getting wind of this, you hear? She still gets frightened sometimes."

Etta walked around the table and put her hand on his shoulders. "She won't find out from us, Dale. Promise."

There seemed to be this whole conversation without words going on between the three lycanthropes in the room that Jo Jo and I weren't privy to. Once again, I felt an expanse between Cal and I that moments earlier we'd bridged. But I had bigger problems than a doomed relationship. "Etta, I think our blood work is the place to start. I hate to ask, but could you sneak a peek at the reports, and the autopsy file while you're at it?"

"Sure." She shrugged. "If you're okay with me destroying the tenuous threat of trust I'd built with Billy Bob by breaking into his files, then I'm okay with it."

"I didn't mean--"

She snorted a laugh. "I'm kidding. He won't catch me, so no harm no foul."

Things I'd learned since arriving at Jo Jo's, Etta used to deal in stolen phones and was, apparently, adept at breaking into places. "You're an interesting girl," I told her.

Cal shook his head. "You have no idea."

"You hush your mouth, Cal Rivers," Etta said.

"WE SHOULD ALSO GO TALK to some of Luke's friends."

"I'll go with you," Cal said.

"No. I don't think they'll open up to me if you're there."

"If they have the same proclivities as their buddy, I don't feel comfortable letting you go off to meet them on your own."

"Then it's a good thing that you're not in charge of me, so letting me or not letting me do anything is not in your job description."

Dale grunted. "I like this one."

"I like her, too," Cal said, "which is why I'm worried. "I'm sorry if I overstepped."

"Forgiven." I looked at Jo Jo. "How about if Jo Jo comes with me, and Cal, you go with Etta."

"And me?" Dale asked.

I sniffed. "You're one of Doc's oldest and dearest friends, right? You can go with Etta and Cal and run interference, maybe get him to tell you a little something about the case that's not in the reports."

"I think it's a pretty good plan," Cal said. "You would have made a good detective."

"I much prefer broken engines to broken people." I stood up. "So, we should get going." I patted my back pocket. "But first, you said you have my phone."

"And clothes," he said.

He went back to his room. I resisted the urge to follow him. When he came back, he had my shirt and jeans folded neatly, with my bra and panties shoved between them, the way I'd placed them the night before. My phone was on top.

He handed them over. "Here you go."

"Thanks."

"It's one-thirty now. Let's agree to meet in two hours at the Sheriff's station for our statements regardless of what we find out," Cal said.

I gave him a quick nod. "Okay. Two hours."

"Good luck," he said.

"You, too."

"Do you guys want us to leave the room?" Etta asked. "Because if I have to hear about Cal's dick again--"

"Etta!" I exclaimed.

She smirked. "Just saying."

"Uhm, okay, let's go, Jo Jo."

He grabbed his phone and keys. "Gladly. We're taking my truck, though, since yours is a piece of crap."

I didn't bother to argue with him because a) it was true, and b) I would die of shame if I spent one more second in the lycanthropes' presence than necessary.

"Two hours," Cal called after me.

I waved at him with the back of my hand as I rushed out the door. "Two hours," I agreed.

"MY TRUCK WOULD HAVE HELD TOGETHER," I groused.

"Don't be grumpy because you got called out on your sexy talk." Jo Jo chuckled. "Which needs a little work, by the way."

"Says you." I crossed my arms over my chest and leaned back in the seat. "It was working just fine until we were interrupted."

"A few more minutes and your little dalliance would have stunted my growth."

"Emotional growth? Maturity?" Besides, there had been nothing little about Cal's dalliance, like, not at all.

"Funny," Jo Jo said. "On a serious note, are you doing okay?"

"It's nice of you to ask. Truth is, I'm not and I am. I know I should be horrified that Luke is dead, especially after seeing him. I should feel grief. This was a man I've known for as long as I can remember, and even if I didn't love him, I should feel sad. But I don't. I feel rage and shame and hate and...regret. What if he had done something like this to my sister. You know Michele went to the same parties as Luke and his buddies. What if he--"

"But he didn't," Jo Jo said, his grip tightening on the steering wheel. He kept his eyes steady on the road. "As soon as I saw what the pictures were, I looked for her in the album."

"What would you have done if you'd found her?"

Jo Jo's lips thinned into an almost feral grimace. "I would have deleted them."

Relief washed through me. Michele hadn't earned Jo Jo's loyalty, but I was glad she had it. "You know, I think a certain werewolf has a crush on you," I said, neatly pivoting the conversation.

Jo Jo raised a brow. "I've seen Dale checking out my ass."

I had to close my mouth when it dropped open in shock. "You've got to be kidding!"

"I certainly am," Jo Jo said.

"That would have been an awkward conversation to have with his wife."

"No kidding." He quickly glanced at me before turning his attention back to driving. "I've given up on Michele."

"Good. You deserve better than a girl with one foot in and one foot out."

"No, worries," he said. "So, where do you want to head first."

"Jackson." Jackson Smart had always been nice to me. An easy guy, who did things like volunteer at the senior center. Luke used to equate Jackson's community works with "drumming up business" for his dad's funeral parlor. "I think he's the most likely to give us information. We may have to hint at things that Luke did at his parties. His reaction will tell us a lot about whether he knew or not."

SMART & SONS FUNERAL HOME was on the northside of town near the Community Christian Church, a nonde-nominational church, and the only one in Peculiar. The interior of the funeral home smelled like powder scented room spray and death. I supposed with a business like theirs, it couldn't be helped. Alice Smart, Jackson's mom, walked out of her office wearing a knee length gray pinstripe dress that fit her curvy figure. She dabbed at her eyes, heavy with black liner and false eye lashes. The Smarts were otters, one of only two families in town that

I knew of, which made them proficient swimmers, even in human form. Jackson had competed on a traveling team our junior year, but when scouts began to look at him like an Olympic hopeful, the Tri-State Council had forced him to quit. It wasn't all that unusual for them, as our governing body, to interfere if they thought something we were doing might draw the wrong kind of attention to our kind--meaning, any kind of attention.

When Alice saw me, sympathy colored her expression, "Oh, my poor dear, she said. Terrible tragedy today. Just terrible. I know how close you two were."

"Thanks, Mrs. Smart. Is Jackson around?"

"Of course, of course. I'm sure you want to talk with him. He's understandably upset, but he insisted on working today. He's such a good boy. Mary Ann has asked him to be a pallbearer." She leaned in conspiratorially. "You know, when Doctor Smith releases young Luke."

Mary Ann was Luke's mother. I couldn't believe they were already planning the funeral. "Isn't this all a little fast?"

"Oh, Jonathan and Mary Ann are devastated. The sooner they can bury their son, though, the sooner they will start the healing."

I wondered if that line was in the brochure. "I'm sure it will take them some time to grieve."

"Of course." She gave me a somber nod. "I'll admit, I was surprised when Mary Ann called this afternoon, but I think she just needed to reach out to someone. I'm an easy choice. We've been friends since high school." She jutted her chin forward and forced a smile. "Now, you were saying about Jackson? Oh, that's right. You asked if he was here. He's cleaning in the viewing room. I'll just send him out."

Jo Jo, who'd hung back at the door, said, "I don't even think she noticed I was here."

"She's pretty manic," I agreed as he joined me inside.

"More like shallow. I don't rate on Alice Smart's matter-meter," Jo Jo said.

"She's not important," I replied. "However, I wonder how much the sheriff told Luke's parents. Alice doesn't seem to know I found his body. I wonder if Mary Ann knows."

"I'm sure the sheriff will be keeping the details under wraps until the investigation gains traction," Jo Jo said. "He's got to know that if people find out that you and Cal were involved, the town is going to go nuts."

I didn't even want to think about what kind of war we'd have on our hands if people started jumping to the wrong conclusions.

Jackson walked into the lobby. He had short hair the color dark chocolate, and he wore a pinstripe suit in a similar shade to his mother's dress. His face registered surprise when he saw Jo Jo standing next to me.

"Mom didn't say you were here, too," Jackson said.

Jo Jo shrugged. "Dakota didn't feel up to driving." It was a small lie that I could live with.

"Your mom said that Mary Ann called already about Luke."

Jackson nodded. "Yeah. I just can't believe it. Do you know what happened?"

"I was hoping you would," I said. "Is there anything you can tell me?"

"The last time I seen him was last night." His gaze wandered as if in thought. Then he said, "When you took off with that werewolf, Luke got real angry. We all went back to my house when the sheriff kicked us off Jo Jo's property." Jackson sounded tired, not angry.

"Who all went back with you?"

"The whole gang. Luke had insisted that he was going to kill someone if he didn't numb the pain." Jackson winced. "I shouldn't have said that." He clasped his hands, his eyes darting away from my gaze. "Luke could be like that sometimes. Impulsive."

That was one word for him. "Jackson, uhm, do you know if Luke was taking any drugs?"

He startled at the question, but then shook his head. "Why do you ask?"

I didn't want him getting suspicious, so I feigned worried ex-girlfriend. "He'd been a little erratic the past couple of months. It was like he'd turned into another person. I thought he might be taking something. It would explain so much."

Jackson's voice grew soft and quiet, "I can't really talk about this here." He gestured with this head toward the back. "But I'd had a few worries, too. Luke had begun running around with integrators from some of the neighboring towns and bringing them out to my house."

"Do you know their names?"

"Some of them," Jackson said. "You might ask Michele. She was pretty chummy with one or two of them."

My heart sunk. "I will do that."

I walked up to Jackson and took his hand for this next part. "I'm sorry about Luke. More than I can say." I was sorry he was a low life scum bag, I thought, who'd tricked me into thinking he was a decent person. "I know he was one of your best friends." I waited until Jackson's gaze dropped down to mine before proceeding. "I hate to ask, but I have to know. Had you ever heard of him doing anything with...uhm, other girls at these parties?"

Jackson looked genuinely confused, which was both disappointing and affirming. "I never saw him hook up with anyone. All he ever talked about was you." Jackson hadn't known about Luke's sadistically perverse dealings. He hadn't known his best friend was a rapist.

"That's comforting to hear," I said. As if an afterthought, I asked, "Can you text me the integrators names that you remember?" I frowned. "I need to get a better picture of what Luke had been going through lately. And maybe some of them can help with closure."

"Of course, D. Anything you need," Jackson said. "Oh, and Jack Trevors came out to the house last night. He told Luke that his parents wanted him to come home. This was early in the evening, and Luke sent him packing, so it's probably not important." He turned to Jo Jo, his expression full of remorse. "I hope you know that I was just along for the ride last night. I didn't know Luke was going to go full-on riot at your place."

Jo Jo grunted then nodded. "We're cool."

But I wasn't. My frustration with Michele was at a ten. She'd been chummy with integrators. Integrators who had probably brought drugs into town. What other stuff was she keeping from our parents? Worse, what had she kept from me?

CHAPTER ELEVEN

"Well, that was odd," Jo Jo said when we got back on the road.

"You're not kidding." There wasn't much traffic to fight as we made our way down Oak Street, but when I saw the Dwyer's black luxury sedan, I scootched down in the seat, cupping my hand over the left side of my face as the vehicle passed by us toward the funeral home. I blew out the breath I'd held and sat up straight when they were safely out of our sight. "Talk about timing."

"They didn't even look in our direction," Jo Jo said. "You know, I've never been a fan of Luke, but I'm sorry for his parents. Losing someone like that can take a toll."

Jo Jo's mother had disappeared thirteen years ago, and it had turned his father into an unemployed alcoholic. It had taken nine years for Jo Jo to finally find out what had happened to her, and the truth of her death had shaken the town to its core.

"I feel bad for them, too. But I don't know how to be around them knowing what I know. They deserve a moment of peace before the truth of Luke gets around."

Jo Jo ran his hand through his short dark hair. His eyebrow piercings glinted as the afternoon sun shone through the windows. "Do you want to talk to Michele next?"

"She's still babysitting," I said. "I'll grill her tonight at home." Besides, if Jo Jo was through with her, there was no sense in forcing him to be around her.

His shoulders relaxed. "Okay, then, where to next?"

"We've got one hour before I have to be at the sheriff's. We know the Dwyers are not at the store, so we should check if Jack Trevors is working today." I clicked my teeth with my tongue. "If not, maybe you can sweet talk old Betty Freedman into giving you his home address."

Betty was ninety years old, but still sassy. She worked the cash register at the grocery store and loved to flirt with the young men who came in to shop.

"I don't think I'm her type," Jo Jo said.

"Don't sell yourself short," I teased like I would a younger brother. "Every guy under the age of sixty is her type."

Jo Jo ignored me. "I think Trevors rents an apartment down by the lakefront. Or used to, anyhow."

"If Jack isn't there, we should track down Eric. He has

been working for his dad at the store lately, ever since his Uncle Elbert got the blood clot in his leg."

Mom had told Dad that Doc Smith ordered Elbert to take it easy. If the old opossum didn't take care of himself until the clot resolved, he'd have a stroke. "Okay, then, grocery store then general store."

My phone rang. Cal's name came up on the screen. I swiped a little too eagerly to accept the call. "Hey, Cal. You're on speaker with Jo Jo and me."

"Hey," he said back. "Checking in."

"Did you find out anything at Doc's?"

"Ketamine," Cal said, his voice sounded strained. "What we had in our system would have taken down an elephant. It could have killed you, Dakota. When we find this guy, I'm going to give him a big dose of my foot right up his ass."

"Wow." My heart fluttered into my throat. "Isn't that one of those date rape drugs?"

"Yes," he snarled.

"Where in the world would someone even get ketamine?"

"Veterinarians can order it," Cal said.

"I can't see Matt Connors, who is our only vet in town, ordering a bunch of ketamine in for recreational use." I shook my head. "He's a middle-aged father of two young boys. He wouldn't sell illicit drugs on the side."

127

"You'd be amazed at the type of people who would sell drugs," Cal said. "The same with those who kill. If the situation is right, people can be motivated to do all kinds of terrible acts."

I nodded. "You're right." Our previous town judge, someone who had been a part of the community his whole life, had turned out to be a serial killer. And, until he was caught, he had appeared the epitome of upstanding.

"Ludlow Davis is Matt's cousin. He works for him at the clinic sometimes," Jo Jo said. "He was out at my house last night with the rest of Luke's mob."

"Ludlow? He's not very bright. How is he going to figure out how to get ketamine past Matt?"

"He's an idiot," Jo Jo agreed.

"Well, it's only a possibility," I said. "Did you manage to get a look at the autopsy report?"

"Unfortunately, Billy Bob hasn't finished, yet. He told Etta it would be a two-day work up."

"She didn't tell him we were working our own investigation, did she?"

"No," Cal said. "She was discreet. I think Billy Bob was happy to have her interested in his work."

Cripes. I hoped our poking around didn't drive Doc and Etta farther apart.

"Does he have any guesses as to how Luke died?" Besides an obvious mauling.

"There is no clear cause of death at this point. What about you guys?"

"Luke's mom is already planning his funeral," I said, slightly aghast. "And Jackson said that Luke had been acting different and bringing integrators into town for parties. When I asked him about the drugs, he acted cagey. I think he knows something, but not about the women."

"You certain," Cal asked.

"As certain as I can be without actually knowing."

Jo Jo turned down North Street toward Dwyer's Market. "I believe him," he said. "For what it's worth."

"We're pulling into the market to see if Jack Trevors is working today. Talk soon," I said.

"Dakota," Cal said. "Stay safe."

His concern for me made me smile. "I will. You stay safe, too."

Jo Jo put the truck in park and pressed his hand against his chest. "Hey! What about me?"

"Goodbye." Cal hung up.

I smirked. "I'll protect you, tiger. Don't you worry."

Jo Jo laughed. He leaned forward in his seat, suddenly, and

looked across the parking lot. He gestured at a woman with dark hair and sunglasses ducking into the store. "Is that Ronnie?"

I squinted at the back of the woman as she entered but it was hard to tell at this distance and angle. "Let's go find out."

WE HAD PERFORMED a fast search of the aisles for any signs of Jack or Veronica, and unfortunately, had found nothing. The store only had a few customers roaming around, so they wouldn't have gotten lost in the shuffle. Time to put Plan B for Betty Freedman to work. Betty, the ninety-year-old buxom blonde bob cat shifter who should have been a cougar, was working the cash register at the checkout line. We waited for the one customer in her line to finish and leave before we approached her.

"Hi, Betty."

She looked at me with my empty hands and no cart, and said, "Can I help you?"

I grabbed a pack of gum and put it up on the conveyor belt. "Uhm, yes. Do you happen to know if Jack Trevors is working today?" I asked as I watched her drag the gum over the scanner."

"I don't think so," she said addressing me but craning her neck to look around me in order to give Jo Jo the once over. See, I'd told him that every guy was her type. "At least, I haven't seen him." She held up the gum. "Do you want this in a bag?"

"No." I took the gum and put it in my pocket.

"That'll be three dollars and twenty-nine cents," she said.

Jayzus, I must have picked the gum laced with gold flecks. I gave her a five. "Did you see Ronnie Talbert come in a few minutes ago?"

"I did," she said, handing me back my change.

"Where did she go?"

"How in the world do I know?" She transferred her gaze away from Jo Jo to me and gave me a sour look. "She hasn't checked out, if that helps."

"Thanks, Betty." I shook my head at Jo Jo. "Trevors is not here, but Ronnie still might be. Let's take a look around. You start walking the front going left to right, and I'll walk the back going right to left."

"On it," Jo Jo said, and we split up.

I stopped at each aisle and glanced down for a second before moving on. As I neared the center of the back, I passed the "employees only" double doors near the public restrooms. What if Veronica had gone into the bathrooms?

I opened the women's door. The teal-green bathroom smelled of lemon detergent. There were a few crumpled paper towels at the base of the trash can, dry, so they had been there a while. "Ronnie? Are you in here?" I asked as I passed each stall. Only one was locked.

A sniffle alerted me to an occupant.

"Veronica? Are you okay?"

"Go away," she said.

"What's wrong?"

"Are you deaf?" she uttered with despair. "Leave me alone."

I went inside the open stall next to her locked one and climbed up on the toilet and looked over the top. She sat on the toilet with her pants up not down, holding a box of tissue. "Why don't you come on out, so we can talk?"

"Christ, Dakota!" Mind your own flippin' business!" Veronica shot up from the toilet, and I saw she had a bruise on her right cheek and a cut on her lip, right before she smacked me in the face with her palm.

I cried out as I slipped off the stool seat, my right foot falling inside the bowl soaking my boot in toilet water. I heard her stall door slam open and the sound of her feet running out of the restroom.

"Son of a beef eater!" I yanked, but the toe of my boot was stuck in the hole. I used both hands to pull on my leg. After three hard yanks, using my free foot for leverage, my boot came loose, and I tumbled out the stall door onto the restroom tiles, taking at hard fall onto my butt

My ankle felt a little tender when I put pressure down on it, but I took off after Veronica as fast as I could hobble. The employee doors were still swinging when I came out of the bathroom, so I went inside after her.

Wooden pallets stacked with cardboard boxes and shrink wrapped littered the warehouse area. So, this is where they took in new goods. Some of the skids were unwrapped with missing boxes, presumably used to stock empty shelves in the store.

I held myself perfectly still, to listen for any movement. *Come on, Veronica, come out, come out, wherever you are.*

When she didn't make a peep, I texted Jo Jo. *Come back to the stock room. Veronica is here.*

Something metal clatter toward the back and I heard quick footfalls. "Gotcha," I said and limped in that direction. Veronica might not be guilty of killing Luke, but she was guilty of something.

Thanks to my twisted ankle, Jo Jo caught up to me. "Where?" he asked.

I pointed toward the east side. Bay doors opened, and daylight poured inside. "She's getting away!"

"You stay put," Jo Jo said. "I'll get her."

He took off running. A roaring sound cut through the stockroom, echoing off the walls. It almost sounded like a growl. I'd heard it before, but where?

I hopped on one foot most of the way in time to see

Veronica take off on a four-wheeler as Jo Jo shouted for her to stop.

"Oh," I said. "Oh." That's what I'd heard the night before when Cal and I'd been shot full of ketamine. That was the growly sound. It had been four-wheelers, more than one.

Jayzus, we weren't just looking at one murderer. There had to be at least two people who knew what had happened to Luke.

"YOU NEED to get ice on that ankle," Jo Jo said. He'd helped me out to the truck. "I'd take off your boot and have a look, but I know where it's been." He wrinkled his nose at me.

"The toilet was clean."

"There's no such thing as a clean toilet, I don't care how much sanitizer gets used."

"Fine," I told him. I called Cal. He answered on the first ring. "I sprained my ankle," I said before he could even say, hello.

"I told you to be careful. Who do I have to take down?"

"Veronica Talbert. She sucker-smacked me in a toilet stall."

There was a long pause, then Cal said, "I'm not sure I want to know. Do you need to see the doctor?"

"Yes," Jo Jo said as I said, "No."

I rolled my eyes. "Probably."

"I'll wait for you," Cal said.

"We're supposed to be at the police station in half an hour." My ankle throbbed, and my toes felt squishy. "I also need a new pair of shoes."

"I think once that boot comes off, you won't be wearing another one for a couple of days," Jo Jo said.

I snarled at him. "Have you always been such a pessimist?"

He smiled as he put the truck into drive. "Yep."

To Cal, I said, "We're on our way."

CHAPTER TWELVE

*M*y ankle hurt like a beast by the time we'd turned onto Doc Smith's road. Jo Jo's truck didn't bounce as badly as mine, but each time we hit a small dip in the road, the pain intensified.

"Uhng," I groaned.

"Hang in there," Jo Jo said.

Cal stood out front, anxiously bouncing on his toes, looking ready to pounce.

Jo Jo grinned. "You're hero."

"Shut up." I punched his arm. Cal had the passenger door open before Jo Jo could put the truck in park.

"Swing your feet out," he said, his blue eyes focusing on my wet booted foot. He supported my calf, making sure the injured ankle was elevated. "Put your arms around my neck, and I'll lift you out."

"Okay." As he wrapped his arms around me, I felt mildly euphoric. "Hey, there," I said when we were nose to nose.

"Hey, there, yourself." He gave me a crooked smile. "Your nose is swelling."

"What?" I'd been so focused on my ankle that I hadn't worried about my face where Veronica had smacked. I touched the tip. "Does it look bad?"

"You're making it work."

Jo Jo got out of truck and opened the door for me as Cal carried me past reception to one of the exam rooms.

He set me on the padded exam table. Etta stuck her head in the room. "Billy Bob will be here in a minute. Get her boot off if you can." Jo Jo assertion that no toilets were clean had bugged me. Before Cal reached down to undo the laces, I said, "Maybe you should get gloves."

"Just in case there's any evidence on it?"

"No, just in case there's any poop on it. It was jammed pretty hard into that toilet bowl."

Cal laughed, loud and rich. "Thank you for the warning." He grabbed two gloves from a box on the sink counter and deftly pulled them on.

God, his eyes in the fluorescent lighting looked jewel-toned, even more so against his lightly bronzed skin. Oh, man, and the way his t-shirt stretched tight against his chest and abs made my mouth water. Lord have mercy, for the first time, I understood Michele's impulsivity. Cal Rivers was going to be my undoing.

He noticed me looking at him, so I said, "You're pretty good at getting those things on. Like a pro."

"This isn't my first time gloving up." He smiled and raised both hands like a surgeon. "The doctor is in."

My pulse quickened. "Oh, you like playing doctor, huh?"

"Do you?" He asked, snapping the latex at the wrist of his glove. He winced at the slight sting it must have caused, and I giggled.

"I could be persuaded. Maybe we could start with a simple exam."

He moved in close. "And where shall we start first, Miss Thompson."

My ankle pulsed with pain and my nose had started to thrumb, but it was my lips that needed his attention. I pointed to them. "We could start here."

"The patient is always right," Cal said. He bent down, his lips brushing softly over mine as a zing of pleasure zipped through me. I placed my palms on his chest as he moved in to kissed me with such sweet tenderness I thought I would burst. I opened for him and took his lower lip between my teeth and gently nibbled. His growl of appreciation spurred me to bite him a little harder.

"Christ, woman," he groaned as he pulled back from me. "I didn't think nice girls liked to bite."

I giggled again. "Who says I'm nice?"

"Everyone," said Etta as she poked her head in again. "Now put it back in your pants. Billy Bob is on his way."

Cal straightened up, but it was easy to see that his jeans were the only thing restraining his erection from pointing at me again.

"Sorry," I mouthed.

"I'm not," he said aloud. He grabbed two more gloves and shoved them in his back pocket. "For later."

My mouth went dry thinking about later, as he unlaced my boot and eased it off. He was just getting to my sock when the doc knocked.

"Can I come in?" Doc asked from behind the closed door.

I blushed. Had he heard us as well? "Sure. Come on in." Nothing to see here...now.

He had his long silver hair pulled away from his face. Since he'd gotten rid of his dread locks, I wasn't sure I'd ever seen him with it down around his shoulders, but I was sure he'd be a sight to behold. His gray eyes swirled as he gave me a questioning look. "Cal says you twisted your ankle."

"Yep." I pointed to my naked foot. "That side."

Doc Smith smiled. "I figured." He put on gloves and touched the inside then the outside of my ankle. I winced and retracted from him when he pressed just above the outer ankle bone. "Okay. Can you move it for me?"

I carefully extended my toes down then up and side to side. "It hurts, but yes."

"The swelling's not too bad at this point," Doc said, "but it's going to get that way if we don't get you treated. Do you want me to call your mom?"

"No," I said faster than I should of.

Doc gave me a suspicious appraisal. "Why not?"

"Because I'm an adult now," I told him. "She doesn't need to know everything that happens to me."

Doc took off one of his gloves and felt my forehead. "Are you feeling all right?"

"Fine. You know, except the ankle."

"And what about your nose?"

"I whacked it on a door," I said. My eyes widened at how easy the lie had spilled from my lips. What in the world? This was not me. I didn't keep things from my mom. I didn't lie to people I'd known, loved, and respected my whole life. It was like someone had come along and gave me a personality transplant. I must have looked like I was internally freaking out, because Cal went around the other side of the exam table and took my hand.

"It's been a difficult day," Cal said. "Neither of us are feeling much ourselves."

Doc nodded. "I was worried that might be the case. I was planning to tell you both later, but now is as good a time as any. I detected large amounts of ketamine in your blood plasma. It can have some strange side effects until it's completely out of your system."

"Like what?"

"It can dull pain receptors, cause mild euphoria, memory gaps, and make you feel foggy brained when it is leaving your system."

"I can certainly feel the pain," I told him, but I have had some euphoria and foggy brain. "Can it make me act out of character?"

"Only at the height of the drug effect, and as long as you aren't using it chronically, those changes are not permanent."

Well, I guess I couldn't blame my racy banter on drug use. "Could this prove that Cal and I aren't responsible for Luke's death?"

Doctor Smith sighed. He looked tired and weary as he sat down on a nearby rolling chair. "That's where it all gets a little tricky." He rolled himself to the sink drawer and pulled out a syringe and a small rubber-topped bottle of clear liquid. "I shouldn't be telling you all this, but Chavvah, through Brother Wolf, is certain Cal, and by default, you, had nothing to do with Luke's death."

"Of course, we didn't."

"What's the problem, Billy Bob?" Cal asked.

"Between liver temp and livor mortis, I can say with some certainty that Luke died between ten and eleven, less than two hours after you went off into the woods. The problem is, I can't say with any certainty when you two were drugged."

"That's just dumb. How can anybody believe we killed Luke then set ourselves up by placing his body and us in the one place Cal isn't allowed?"

Cal squeezed my hand. "They could say we staged it to throw suspicion off us to mislead the investigation."

I scoffed so hard it hurt my throat. "That's ridiculous."

"I agree," Doc said. "But I've seen a lot of unbelievably boneheaded criminals over the years. This wouldn't be the craziest plan in the bunch. Close, but not quite."

"Have you asked Matt Connors about his ketamine supply at his clinic?" I asked.

"He's looking in to it." Doc's suspicious gaze landed on me.

I tried not to shrink under his scrutiny. "Ketamine is an animal tranquilizer. It's not hard to think Doctor Connor is the logical choice for supplying the drug."

"Uh huh," Doc said, tipping up the bottle and sucking up the contents into his syringe. "You have anything to add, Cal?"

"Nope."

Doctor Smith frowned. "Fine, but if you two are getting any ideas about trying to find Luke's killer, I would caution you against it." He flicked his gaze to me. "You know that we have your back. Your parents, Chav and Me, Sunny and Babe, and Willy Boden. We are all working hard to make sure this doesn't come down on you."

"I'm not worried about me," I said. I'd never even considered I might be a real suspect. "But Cal..."

"So, are you two a thing now?" Doc asked.

"I don't know what we are," I said honestly, "But I do know we're not murderers."

Doc frowned at Cal. "We'll talk about this later." The way he said it made my heart hurt. Would he and Chav, as the leaders of the werewolves forbid Cal from seeing me? Could he do that?

"Anything you have to say to Cal, you can say with me in the room," I said.

Doc raised his brow at Cal. "Hold her ankle still for me."

When Cal did, he plunged the needle into my ankle and depressed the plunger. It burned as if he'd pumped me full of rubbing alcohol, but only for a few seconds. By the time he withdrew the needle, the pain was only a dull ache.

"What is that miracle in a bottle?" I asked as I wiggled

my toes. "Oh, it's spit, right? Lycan mouth juju as Sunny calls it."

"It's been sterilized and combined with lidocaine and a steroid for rapid relief. Even so, take it easy for a few days," Doc said. "You can walk on it as long as it's wrapped but no running or jumping."

He took a bandage from a shelf under the counter and wrapped my foot. "You both better get down to the Sheriff's to give your statements. Better to arrive on your own than in custody. And then maybe you both should lay low until Cal has been cleared of wrong doing. Chav said there was a lot of grumbling at Sunny's Outlook this morning, and Babel has had his share of phoned in complaints. If people see the two of you together, it will fuel the bigotry. Don't give them a reason to make things worse."

It made me angry, but I nodded. I had no intention of laying low, but it wouldn't serve any purpose to argue with him.

When the doc got ready to leave the room, I asked, "Do you know how Luke died?"

"I think so, but I need a few more tests to confirm my theory."

"Was it from a shifter attack? His face..."

"The wounds," Doc said, "happened after he died."

CHAPTER THIRTEEN

*C*al took me back to Jo Jo's so I could get my truck. The extra clothes I kept for Linus in the toolbox also had a pair of tennis shoes in there for him. Linus, for a little guy, had slightly bigger feet than me, but the shoes worked. Especially since my right ankle had swelled some. After, I followed Cal into town to the Sheriff's Department. I dreaded running into Tyler after the way he'd acted at the crime scene. I knew the way he acted came from a place of fear, not hate. Taylor had lived for surprises, always trying new adventures, but Tyler, he'd thrived on routine. He never wanted anything to change. Heck, he'd even had a go at Sunny when she'd first come to town. In some ways, I was a little like him. I liked routine as well. It was comforting knowing how the day was going to play out. But after spending even a short amount of time with Cal, I was beginning to see the appeal of exploring the unknown.

There were dozens of cars lining the street leading to the

Sheriff's Department, and even more people, both men and women, standing out on the sidewalks. Jack Trevors, Ludlow Davis, easy to pick out because of his bright red hair, and Madison West stood near the parking lot entrance and when Cal pulled in, Ludlow smacked the hood of his truck. I laid on my horn hard enough to make the chassis vibrate.

Ludlow looked over his shoulder at me and gave me the middle finger. As I approached the parking lot. He sneered, his face full of contempt. He smacked my hood as well. "Traitor!" he bellowed.

"Traitor," Madison West joined in. Soon, a few more voices joined the chant.

I rolled down my window as I passed by. "Screw you, Ludlow! Screw all of you!"

I pulled into a parking space next to Cal, and Eldin Farraday was waiting for us near the back. He waved to me, but before Cal and I could join him, someone hit me in the back with something hard. I whipped around and saw a cracked egg on the ground near my feet.

"Traitor!" I heard again, but I'd gone slightly numb. I grew up with these people and one of them had just egged me.

Cal roared, but he didn't get a chance to act, because, seemingly out of nowhere, my mom appeared. She shook a rolling pin in Ludlow's face. I think I blanched as much as Ludlow did. Madison and Jack must have seen my mom coming because they had both moved far enough away from the meathead that I couldn't see them anymore.

"I swear to all that is merciful I will make your life a living hell if you don't back off, Ludlow Davis." My mom snapped her non-rolling pin fingers in his face. "Right now!" Then she turned on the crowd and shook her kitchen weapon at them. "All of you! You should be plum ashamed of yourselves. This is not how we behave in Peculiar. Get home before you not only shame yourselves, but you put shame on your families." Willy Boden had joined Mom in her uniform with her hand on her weapon, and she stood behind her ready to back whatever play her bestie Ruth wanted to make.

"Your daughter is the one who should be ashamed," someone shouted.

Mom held the rolling pin up higher. "Who said that?" When no one claimed responsibility, Mom shouted. "Cowards! The lot of you. Now get your asses home!"

Several gasps went out among the mob. I gasped as well. Mom rarely uttered a curse word, so you knew she meant serious business when it happened. These folks were fixin' to get an old-fashioned butt whooping if they didn't do as they were told.

And they knew it, because within seconds, the sidewalks were cleared and vehicles were driving away. Mom stalked over to me and started dusting my back, picking small bits of egg shell off my shirt. "Are you okay, baby?"

"I'm okay." Tears threatened to spill over, and I gave her a firm hug.

She held me for a moment, and said, "Be brave." She gave me a motherly swat with the rolling pin on the heinie. "Go in and get it over with. I'll make sure no one messes with you all while you're here."

"Are you going to sit on the front steps and chase people away?" I asked, wiping my eyes.

"If I have to." She smacked the pin against her open palm, and Heaven help the jerk who tries to come after my girl."

Cal stepped up next to me. "Hello, Mrs. Thompson," he said. "That was a pretty bad ass move you made back there."

She adjusted her hair. "I don't suffer fools easily," she said.

"I can see that," he told her.

Eldin joined us. "Man, Ruth, Sheriff Taylor needs to hire you for riot control. You and that rolling pin are a better deterrent than tasers and fire hoses."

Mom gave him an accusing look. "If you all had been doing your job I wouldn't have been put in that situation in the first place."

"Are you going to take the rolling pin to Eldin, now, Mom?" Since she was completely riled up, I kept my tone neutral. "Remember, he's on our side. And it's not his fault some people are stupid."

Mom blinked, her large brown eyes looking a little bewildered and lost. "I'm sorry, Eldin. You come over later, and I'll make it up to you with some apple pie."

"All is forgiven, Ruth." He glanced at me and Cal. "I better get these two inside."

Mom gave me another quick hug. "I love you," she said.

I teared up again. "I love you, too, Mom."

As we walked away from her, Cal leaned in close. "I've got to get me some of this famous pie."

I nudged him with my shoulder. "If you play your cards right."

Inside the police station, John Connelly took me to his desk, and Eldin took Cal to his. I was never so glad my brother Tyler had the day off.

"Here you go, Dakota," John said. "Fill out this witness statement form. The sheriff wants to talk with you and Rivers when you're finished." He gave me a sympathetic glance. "Take your time and try to be as accurate as possible."

Considering I didn't remember much from the time we were drugged until the time I woke up on the Hackenstraw property with a dead body, the form wasn't going to take me much time at all. I watched Eldin interact with Cal for a few seconds. He smiled as he handed Cal the form. Shook his head. Both of them even chuckled once. Maybe Cal would get a fair shake, at least with law enforcement. Doctor Smith most likely faxed over the preliminary reports, at least on our blood work, so they'd be nuts to think Cal had been with it enough to kill Luke. At the very least it would give a strong case for reasonable doubt.

I noticed their white board, where they registered arrests and complaints was covered with a black sheet. I kept looking up at it as I filled in all the questions, dotted my i's, crossed my t's. There must be something of interest under there or the sheriff wouldn't have bothered to throw something over it before we came in.

I leaned over to Connelly. "Hey, John, what's up with the cloth?"

"Not allowed to say." His eyes danced to the board and back to me. "Sheriff's orders."

"So, you don't know?"

"I know. I'm just not allowed to say." He shook his head. "Don't try to bait me, Dakota. I live with the toughest interrogator in town. If Selena can't get it out of me, you have no shot."

Wow. He hadn't even told his wife. It had to be relevant to the case, then. John Connelly was a squirrel shifter, and his wife Selena was a bear shifter. They were one of the predator-prey exceptions. They had two children now, and I wondered how they managed to make it work. Especially on the full moon.

"Do you and Selena ever have any issues?"

He frowned. "Like what?"

"You know, with her being a bear and you being a squirrel."

"Nope."

I cocked my head sideways. "Do you still run on the Hackenstraw property?"

"Full moons, yes."

"So, not together."

"Nope."

"Do you ever worry she might attack you or the kids on a full moon?" His kids were squirrel shifters like him.

"This conversation is making me uncomfortable," John said. He adjusted the height of his chair and swiveled back and forth as if testing it.

"Oh." I sat back. "I'm sorry. I wasn't trying to be rude." I glanced over at Cal who looked up at me from his clipboard, smiled, and gave me a finger wave. I smiled back.

"I get it," John said. "You're worried what it means if you date someone like Rivers over there."

I wagged my fingers at him to shush him. "Keep your voice down," I whispered. "Lycanthropes have super good hearing."

"I'm no expert, but I will tell you, Selena and I were late for a full moon one month and we both turned in the house. This was before the kids, of course, but nothing happened. I mean, the furniture was trashed, and Selena had dug all the food out of the fridge during the night, but we woke up next to each other without a single scratch or bite mark. The only reason we haven't tried it again, is because of the kids. Not because I think she would hurt them, but because one of the other shifters might. I think there is an instinct even when we go into our animal's natural state that tells us when we're around the people we care about. Love. I don't know if it's like that with the lycanthropes, but you shouldn't be afraid to find out."

I rapidly blinked, reassessing everything I'd ever thought about John Connelly. Because he was a squirrel shifter, he was the butt of a lot of nut jokes, and sometimes it could be hard to take him seriously, especially since his wife, while nice, was the biggest gossip in town. Even so, his still waters ran deep. "Thank you, John. I appreciate your candor." This also meant, that maybe Cal and I running together on a full moon had not been a fluke. We knew each other, even when we didn't.

He nodded. "You about finished?"

I printed my named, dated the form, then signed on the line below. "Finished," I said.

"I'll let the sheriff know."

CHAPTER FOURTEEN

I'm not sure what I expected but being placed in a small white room, with a white table, two chairs on one side and single one on the other, was not it. I was surprised they hadn't separated Cal and me. "Do you think they put us together hoping we would say something incriminating to each other?"

"Probably," he said. He pointed to a camera in the corner of the ceiling.

I stared at it for a second then turned my attention to a closed manila envelope sitting in the center of the table. "What do you think that is?"

"More smoke and mirrors," Cal said. "It's a ploy to make us think they have incriminating evidence. You know, to rattle us."

"It's working." I was rattled as all get out.

Cal slid his palm into mine and interlaced our fingers. "We didn't do anything wrong."

"Said every wrongful conviction," I retorted. I squeezed his hand. "You see stuff like this on TV, but you can't know how nerve-racking it is until you're in the hot seat."

"I get the idea that the last thing anyone in this town wants to do is find you guilty, of anything. You have a lot of folks around here on your side."

"What makes you say that?"

"I've been around this town long enough to hear things. Chavvah asked your mom about having nine children a few weeks ago, and your mom told her that if she didn't have you, she probably would have been put in a mental institution for tired moms years ago."

"I do what I can to help."

"Jo Jo told me you're a great mechanic, as good as your dad. And I've seen the way everyone treats you. You don't get that kind of respect because you're unreliable." Cal rubbed the back of my hand with his free one. "I've even heard some refer to you as perfect."

"I don't want to be perfect," I confessed. "Doing the right thing all the time is a lot of work."

"If it was easy, everyone would do it." He nudged me with his shoulder and smiled.

"You know I'm not perfect, right? Because, if that's why

you want to date me, we should probably just end things now."

He took his hand out of mine. "Well, shoot, I feel like I've been sold a bill of goods."

"Har har." I grabbed his hand back. "You're in this now with me whether you like it or not."

"Then it's a good thing I like it."

Sheriff Taylor entered the room. He put his phone down on the table and pushed a red record button displayed on the screen. "Sheriff Sydney Taylor entering room at four p.m. on March twenty-second. Callum David Rivers and Dakota Augusta Thompson are both seated in the room."

Cal raised a brow at me and mouthed the word, "Augusta?"

I crossed my eyes at him. "It's a family name."

"Are you two done playing footsy?" Sheriff Taylor asked using his most official and scary tone.

Cal's foot, which had been up against mine, moved an inch or two away. However, he kept a hold of my hand. "Good afternoon, Sheriff," he said respectfully. "What can we do for you?"

"I've done some digging on you, Mr. Rivers. You were in the army for four years, and a member of the military police corps for the last two years of service. After you were discharged, you signed up for the Oklahoma Highway Patrol Academy, then spent the next several years in law enforcement." The sheriff settled himself back in a chair across from us. He tapped the envelope expectantly.

"All that is true," Cal replied. "You got me. I was a law-abiding citizen."

"Until," the sheriff continued, "three years ago when you, suddenly quit your job, without notice I might add. The very same night a wanted fugitive was mauled to death by a wild animal." The sheriff opened the envelope and pulled out a photo of a scruffy man with graying hair who had deep slashes across his face and chest, also with a good portion of his throat torn.

I let go of Cal's hand and pressed my palm into my roiling stomach. "I..." I vomited across the table and the photo.

The sheriff and Cal both jumped up to avoid splatter of mostly bile as I puked again. The sheriff pressed a red button on the wall, and Connelly rushed inside the door, his gun drawn, with Farraday on his tail, taser at the ready.

"Sorry, sorry," I muttered when the wave of nausea passed. "It just hit me."

Eldin made a face when he saw the sick all over the table surface. "I'll go get some cleaning supplies.

Cal's expression hardened. "I think she needs some water."

WHO LET THE WOLVES OUT?

"I'm fine," I said feeling much better than I had moments before. "It passed."

Sheriff Taylor rose to his feet and shook his head. "We're not staying in this room."

The sharp stench of stomach acids burned my nostrils. "I'm sorry," I said again.

"The pictures were disturbing, Dakota." The sheriff managed to look contrite. "I'm sorry you had to see them."

I nodded. Only, it wasn't the pictures that had made me sick. "I think it's a side effect of being drugged I told him. I feel okay now."

Cal stood up and moved to put himself between me and Connelly, who still had his gun drawn. "Can you put that away?"

The sheriff nodded at his deputy. "It's all right, John. I think we're going to take this to my office to finish."

Once Connelly holstered his pistol and departed, Cal said, "Wait." He pulled his shirt off, and while I wasn't opposed to the gun show, his sudden exhibitionism confused me.

Until he pointed at the round scar on his shoulder, then another that he hadn't shown me at the apex of his stomach, and another on his hip. When he turned, there were two more scars near his mid-back. "I didn't know Rick O'Brien was a wanted fugitive when I pulled him over."

"The speeding ticket," I said.

"Yes," Cal acknowledged. "It was a routine traffic stop in the middle of a night shift on a long, lonely stretch of highway north of Tulsa. Until O'Brien opened fire on me at close range. He hit me in the chest first, then in the gut, taking me down to my knees before I could react or protect myself. He pushed his car door open and knocked me down. I have no doubt he planned to kill me, so I did what I had to do to defend myself. My human body was too frail and weak. I shifted to my partial form, and O'Brien put three more bullets from his forty-caliber pistol into me, hitting me in the hip and my back. And I..." His lips thinned as I saw the memory play out in his mind before he said, "I killed him."

"Oh, Cal." My hand had gone to my mouth as if it would somehow cover the horror of what had happened to him.

"How did you survive?" Sheriff Taylor asked.

"I was able to call my leader William Smith before I passed out from blood loss. He sent some medics and a team of cleaners, a group of lycanthropes who specialize in covering these kinds of incidents." He looked at me. "I was nearly dead when they found me, but luckily, lycanthropes heal pretty fast. About five times as fast as humans, so once they got the blood stopped, they were able to safely transport me back to White Rock."

I thought about the magic spit. Therian's healed a little faster than humans, but not by much. The fact that lycans were able to heal at a supernatural speed drove home how different we truly were as species.

Cal continued his story. "The cleaners disposed of his car and took him out to the woods and staged the body. One of them, who was similar in body type to me, wore one of my uniforms to return my patrol car and turn in my resignation letter." Cal put his shirt back on. "I hope you can understand, I didn't want to take his life."

The sheriff nodded. "I believe you, son." He gestured to us. "I needed to confirm the O'Brien incident was you to clear you as a suspect in this case. The claw marks and bites on Luke don't match in size or pattern to the O'Brien mauling. Along with Doctor Smith's reports that you two had been pumped full of ketamine, I think it's safe to say, that you are not responsible for what happened to Luke Dwyer."

THE SHERIFF LET US GO, with a warning to keep a low profile until the investigation had concluded, or at least the fervor about lycanthropic involvement died down. I worried about what might be waiting for us when we got outside, but the sidewalks were still clear, thanks to my mom. Cal walked me to my truck.

"Are we okay?" he asked. "I didn't want you to find out about O'Brien that way."

"I knew you'd been shot, but that man nearly succeeded in killing you," I said. "I'm not okay with that at all."

He hugged me. "Go home and get some rest, then meet me at Jo Jo's"

I had a better idea. "Pick me up at seven. It's time you meet my brother."

"The deputy? Because we've already met."

"Not Tyler," I said. "His twin, Taylor. I think his boyfriend might be able to fill in some of the blanks." Like what the sheriff had covered up on his white board.

"Boyfriend?"

"Deputy Farraday. The officer who interviewed you."

"Huh. Okay," Cal said. He nodded. "It's a plan. Now, go get some rest. I'll pick you up at seven." He kneaded my back as I tilted my chin up to meet his goodbye kiss.

I was a little breathless when it ended. "You know I recently threw up, right?"

"Yeah," he said, his mouth turned up in a wicked grin. "That's why I left out any tongue action."

I smacked his chest. "You're crazy."

"For you," he said.

My pulse fluttered. I was crazy about him, too, and I wanted to tell him so, but Etta's talk about mates and such kept playing in my mind. I could date Cal if I wanted. I could have some fun, which I needed. But I could not get serious. Trouble was, things already felt pretty damned serious to me. Eventually, we'd have to have a long talk about expectations, but right now, I just wanted to go home, brush my teeth, take a bath, and get

an hour or two of sleep in before dinner. "I'm exhausted."
I yawned. "And my bed is calling me."

"That sounds like an invitation. How big is your bed?"

"You show up in my bed, and you're going to end up on
the wrong end of my mom's rolling pin. And make no
mistake, she will totally thrash you."

"I don't doubt it for a second." He chuckled and kissed
me again. "But, you are totally worth it."

CHAPTER FIFTEEN

*M*y truck shook as I drove it the two blocks to our house. Instead of pulling into the driveway, I parked it in the customer lot at the auto shop. The garage doors were open, and my dad was working under the hood of a newer model Chevy Silverado. He walked out to meet me when I got out.

"You're going to have to fix that front end sometime," he said. He wiped the grease from his hands with a rag he always kept in his pocket.

"I know." I gave my truck a wistful look. "She needs a lot of work."

He nodded. "How are you doing?"

"Okay. Have you talked to mom?"

"Yep. I didn't like that kid much, but I'm sorry he's dead."

"I'm not sure I am," I replied honestly.

Dad raised a brow. "Care to elaborate."

"Not really. I've just found out some things today about Luke that makes me regret the months I spent going out with him." I leaned back on my bumper. "I thought you liked him. Mom was over the moon when I told her we were dating."

"You can tell a lot about a man by the way he treats the people around him. I've watched Luke when he thought no one was looking. He was the kind of guy that made others feel small, so he could seem big."

"Why didn't you tell me how you felt?"

"You're a smart girl, Dakota. After all, you're your mother's daughter. I knew you'd figure it out on your own." He gestured toward the house. "By the way, Mary Ann Dwyer is visiting your mom right now, and she brought that Jack Trevors with her."

Crap. What in the world could I say to Mrs. Dwyer that wouldn't sound false or pandering. And why was Jack with her?

As if reading my mind, Dad said, "Mary Ann heard about the incident at the sheriff's. She is insisting Jack give you an apology, along with assurances that nothing like that will happen in the future."

"Why would he agree to that?"

Dad shrugged. "Jobs are scarce in Peculiar. Besides, they are renting him a trailer out at the edge of their property. I suppose he could potentially lose his home as well."

So, he'd moved from the lakefront apartments to a trailer out on the Dwyer's land. Was that significant? Maybe. Maybe not.

I nodded. "Thanks, Dad."

"For what?"

"For warning me."

"One more thing," he said. "Do you know what's going on with Lisa Ann? She's been acting strange since she got home from school."

"You know how she is. She's always danced to the beat of her own hooves. But if you're worried, I'll check on her."

Dad put his hands on my shoulders and kissed my forehead. "You're a good kid, Dakota."

I held back a sigh. "I know."

I crossed the yard between the shop and the house at a leisurely pace. I was in no hurry to speak with Mrs. Dwyer or Jack. I thought it was strange her bringing him to the house, for an apology of all things. The Dwyers really kept their employees under their thumbs. My dad was right, jobs were scarce in town. The fear that the lycans would take jobs from the locals was one of the biggest complaints people had with them in town. But I couldn't imagine being desperate enough to keep a job as a stock boy to put up with this kind of treatment.

The throbbing in my ankle had increased, which meant the lidocaine the doc had shot in there was wearing off. Also, I had rubbed a blister on my heel because of my little brother's ill-fitting shoes. On top of that, I hadn't peed in several hours and my bladder was stretched to capacity. Still, I contemplated running away.

Butch came out the back door about the time I was ready to flip a coin. He gave me a, *you're in trouble*, look, then said, "Mom's been watching you from the kitchen window. She sent me out here to tell you to get your derriere in the house. Her word, not mine."

"I'm coming," I said. My shoulders sagged as I trudged up the stairs on the back porch. "Tell mom I need to run upstairs first to pee."

He rolled his eyes. "Good luck getting Lisa out of the bathroom."

My phone buzzed, but I ignored it as I went inside. Mom met me at the base of the stairs. "Everything go all right with the sheriff?" she asked.

"Yes," I said. "We've been cleared as suspects. The sheriff has evidence to prove Cal wasn't responsible for Luke's wounds. And since I don't have claws or fangs..."

"Good," she said. "Now, hurry up and do what you've got to do. Mary Ann Dwyer would like to speak with you."

"Dad told me." I got one of those bladder twinges that happen when you wait too long. "I really have to go, Mom. I'll be down in a minute." If the tightness across my stomach was any indication, I was about to unleash a river.

"Go," she said. "But don't dally."

"Cross my heart. No dallying."

"COME ON, Lisa. I need in the bathroom now!" I knocked on the locked door again. "Unless you are having a medical emergency, let me in."

"Fine!" my youngest sister said. I heard the door unlock.

I push past her, slammed the door behind me, and beelined for the toilet. "What is going on with you?" I shoved my pants to mid-thigh and sat down. It took a second for the flow to start, but when it did, it just kept going. So much relief!

Lisa sat on the edge of the tub, her eyes red and watery like she'd been crying.

"What's up, buttercup?" I asked as the urine stream became more of a dribble. I wondered if someone could go in to shock by peeing too much.

"Nothing," she said.

"You've been crying."

"I have not." She pivoted her knees away from me and wiped at her eyes with the back of her fist.

"Allergies, huh?"

Lisa rolled her eyes at me.

"Look, you're starting to worry the parents. So, you can either tell me, or you can get grilled by them later."

"I swore not to tell," she said.

"Swore to who?"

"I can't tell."

"Look, I can tell that whatever it is, it's really bothering you. Some secrets are too toxic to keep." I thought about Katrina Wells. "Trust me."

Lisa looked away as I wiped and got my britches pulled back up.

I went to the sink and washed my hands with peach antibacterial soap. The sweet fruity scent always reminded me of summer. "Is this about Bobby Davis?"

"Why do you think it's about Bobby?" Her shoulders tightened around her ears and her body was suddenly rigid.

"Did he hurt you?"

She shook her head but wouldn't meet my gaze. "No. It's not about Bobby, at least not like you're thinking."

"Did someone threaten you?"

"Just drop it," Lisa said. Her back pack was in the tub. She scooped it up. "I hate this house. I hate this family." She glared at me. "And I hate you!"

She flung the bathroom door open and fled the room.

"Well." I blinked in the wake of Hurricane Lisa. She hadn't been the first of my siblings to say they hated me. Emma Ray said it once when she was ten, when I told her she had to clean her room, and Thomas said it to me when I'd walked in on him masturbating. Truthfully, that experience had been traumatic for both of us. He learned to lock the bathroom door after that, and I had learned to knock. Still, hearing her say it had hurt, even if I knew it was a reaction to whatever had Lisa stressed and frightened.

After I brushed my teeth and ran a comb through my hair, I had no more reasons to avoid Mrs. Dwyer. For a brief moment, I considered crawling out a window, but somehow found the courage to face whatever was coming my way. I walked past Lisa and Emma Ray's room. The door was closed. I knocked softly, and said, "Hey, if you want to talk, I'm here."

Lisa didn't scream at me again, so I took that as a good sign.

———

MOM AND MRS. DWYER sat at the table, while Jack Trevor, looking like a naughty schoolboy waiting to see the principal, stood by the sink. His hair was light brown, and his eyes were the color of caramel. I'd never paid that much attention to him, since he hadn't gone to school with me, and while he might have been a pal of Luke's, he'd never hung around with us when Luke and I had dated. I was usually pretty good at picking out the type of therianthrope someone was based on their shared characteristics, but as I looked at Jack, I was confounded.

Mrs. Dwyer stood up when I walked into the kitchen. "Oh, Dakota," she said, clearly distressed. She held out her hands, her freshly manicured nails painted her signature red, and gave me a quick embrace.

"I'm so sorry about Luke," I told her. "I guess you heard, uhm, that I found him."

"It's just awful." She choked on a sob. "I can't believe he's gone. I can't believe we've lost our Luke."

He wasn't my Luke, and he hadn't been for a while. I'd told Mrs. Dwyer as much the day before, but I didn't correct her now. The woman was in mourning and I didn't want to add to her suffering if I could help it. Mostly, because it would have been plain rude. I'd wanted to offer more words of condolence, to say things like, "He'll be missed," or "Everybody loved him," the things you say to make the people left behind feel like the dead mattered, but in Luke's case it would be complete bull.

I tried not to fidget under her intense gaze. "Is there anything I can do for you?"

"I'm so glad you asked," Mrs. Dwyer said. "I was hoping you would sing at Luke's memorial service on Sunday. It's at one in the afternoon at Smart's Funeral Home. Luke had told me about a night you all went out to karaoke. He couldn't say enough about what a beautiful voice you had."

I had sung choir in high school, and I'd won the senior solo. So, when Luke and I first started dating it had been my idea to go to karaoke night in Lake Ozarks. I'd wanted to impress him, so I'd sang, "Angel" by Sarah McLachlan. Totally corn-ball, but I guess I'd accomplished my mission. Luke had been impressed.

Before I could make an excuse to turn her down, like I had a sore throat, or what have you, Mrs. Dwyer said, "Good, I'm so glad that's settled." She cleared her throat. "Now, Jack has something he'd like to say to you."

"Sorry," he muttered like a petulant child.

"Jack," Mrs. Dwyer said, her tone full of warning.

"Sorry," he said louder.

"For," she said.

"For organizing the protestors at the Sheriff's station."

"You organized it?" I crossed my arms defensively. "Why would you do that?"

He shrugged, his gaze flicking back and forth between me and Mrs. Dwyer. "I did it for Luke."

Mrs. Dwyer's voice was high and sharp. "Dakota was the only real bright spot in Luke's life. He would have hated you for this."

Jack's face reddened as if he'd been slapped. "Yes, ma'am," he said.

Mrs. Dwyer nodded her satisfaction. "We have a few more stops to make, so we'll get out of your hair, Ruth. Thank you for your kindness, and for the casserole and pie."

"It is my pleasure, Mary Ann. You shouldn't have to be thinking about meals at a time like this. That's what a community is for."

"And Jonathan and I are so blessed to be in Peculiar. Especially now." She glowered at Jack. "In the meantime, I assure you that this one won't be causing any more problems. Right, Jack?"

He nodded again. "Yes, ma'am."

"Wait," I said. "Jackson Smart said that Jack tried to get Luke to go home last night."

"That's right," Mrs. Dwyer said. "But Luke never did." She pulled a tissue from her purse and wept into it. "I never got to say goodbye. Now, we really must go. Come on, Jack."

I was beginning to feel sorry for Jack. He seemed to be the whipping boy for all the Dwyers.

After they departed, we watched them walk out to Mrs. Dwyer's sedan. Jack opened the passenger door for Mrs. Dwyer then ran around to the driver's side and got in. As they pulled out, I noticed Mom's horrified expression mirrored my own.

"Wow," she said. "Mary Ann is one scary boss lady."

"Truth." I poured myself a glass of water and sat down at the table. "Did you think she was acting strange?"

"Grief can come out in a lot of different ways. She's lost her only child, so why don't we cut her some slack."

"I really don't want to sing at the memorial service."

"That doesn't sound like you, Dakota. You're always the first one to offer help to those in need. Even if you were no longer with the boy, it's the right thing to do. His parents are our friends."

I couldn't explain to her why I didn't want to sing for Luke's service, and it irritated me that she was pushing me to "do the right thing."

I shook my head. "Fine. You win," I said. "I'll sing at the stupid memorial."

"I win?" My mother got a look on her face usually reserved for Tyler or Michele when they did something really ignorant. "Is that what you think? That I want to win? That woman lost her son. Her only child. She won't have another one. And all you can think about is that fact that I've somehow won? I'm so disappointed in you, Dakota. And I don't like the feeling, not one bit."

I sighed, my heart sick with the turmoil brewing inside me. *There are things you don't know. Things I can't tell you*, I wanted to say. Instead, I agreed with her. "I'm disappointed, too, Mom. And I don't like the feeling one bit."

CHAPTER SIXTEEN

hinking about you, Cal texted at five-thirty.
You ok?

I'd been stewing in my room since my dressing down by my mom. I wondered if Michele felt this awful when it happened. Probably not, or she wouldn't keep getting into trouble. *Fine. Wish it was 7 already*, I texted back.

I can come over now. Just say the word.

Better not. Mom in a mood.

Uh oh.

Luke's mom by earlier. Tell you about it tonight.

K. ... What are you wearing?

The question made me giggle. I had put on a pair of harem athletic pants, the stretchy kind with the loose crotch and an oversized green t-shirt after my shower. But

I texted, *A sexy, high-cut chastity belt. Medieval design. Double bolted for added security*.

He sent me a surprise emoji and a laughing emoji. *You're so sexy*.

LOL. That's why the chastity belt. But just in case he thought I was serious or not interested, I added, *Don't worry. I'll bring the keys*.

The heart emoji made me smile so hard my cheeks hurt.

"Time for dinner!" Mom yelled.

Have to go. Talk soon.

Can't wait.

I put my phone away. Thanks to Cal, I was no longer in a funk.

"Dinner!" Mom yelled again.

I rolled my eyes and hopped out of bed. "Coming!" Cripes, what the heck was happening to me? I grabbed my phone again, and texted, *On second thought, come now for dinner*.

You sure your mom won't mind.

No. But I'm willing to chance it if you are.

Be there in a few.

I threw on a spring dress, a white one with pretty yellow flowers on it. I pulled my favorite denim jacket on and put on my cutest tan cowgirl boots, that hit low on the calf and had a slight heel to them. Plus, they were roomy enough to accommodate the bandage on my ankle. I hadn't told Mom or Dad about seeing the doc today, and I felt guilty, just not enough to come clean.

Michele poked her head in my bedroom. "Are you coming down or what?" Then she whistled. "Looking good, sis."

"Thanks. I have a dinner guest on the way."

"Your werewolf?"

"How do you--"

"It is the talk of the town. Besides, I'm the one who gave him your number."

"Oh, yeah, about that..."

She held up a hand. "You can thank me later." She laughed. "I think you're going to have to fight Mom though if you want to leave tonight. She's pretty freaked out about Luke getting killed and you being thrown in the thick of it. It's messing with her usual Zen."

Well, shoot. Mom had been edgy, but so had I, and that's probably why we'd clashed today. Me being in danger had put her on emergency lockdown, but it had made me want to live. Really live. "I'm twenty-four-years-old, Mishy. Mom is going to have to let go a little."

"And you should tell her that." She smiled as if her evil plan was coming together. "Tell her just like that."

"What are you up to?"

She shrugged then sighed. "I'm thinking about leaving Peculiar."

"Are you serious? Why? For what reason?"

"I've been seeing someone, and he wants me to move in with him. In Springfield."

My mouth dropped open as my adrenaline spiked. "You want to become an integrator?"

Michele laughed. "Don't say it like it's a dirty word, Kota." She shook her head. "Look. Springfield is only a few hours away. I have some money saved up to carry my half of the expenses until I can get a job." She frowned at me. "Don't look so forlorn, for Pete's sake. I'll come home so much you won't even miss me."

"Who? Does Mom and Dad know you're dating an integrator?"

"It's Brad Connors. He's going to college there, and when he graduates, he wants to stay in the city. And he wants me with him." She looked so jubilant. Did I really have the right to try and stomp all over her dreams? No. That was our parents' job. "If your happy, I'm happy for you. Brad always seemed like a nice guy."

"Thanks. I am, and he is."

"Speaking of integrators. Tell me what you know about drugs at Jackson Smart's parties."

She averted her gaze and was suddenly fidgety. "I don't know what you mean."

"You're usually a much better liar," I told her.

She smiled. "You threw me off guard with your supportive sister act."

I held out my hand to her. "It's not an act. I'll support whatever you decide."

She gave my fingers a grateful squeeze. "Luke and Ludlow were bringing in club drugs to the parties, not the integrators. Some of Brad's friends, though, were buying them and taking them back to Springfield to up-market sell them at night clubs and frat parties. Brad and I tried some of it once."

"Mishy!"

"I'm fine," she said. "And don't get mad at Brad. It was my idea."

Of course, it had been. "Was it ketamine?"

"It was cut with some ecstasy and GBH, but yes, I'd heard Ludlow bragging about the blend. It made me feel good, but I had some weird hallucinations and it freaked me out. Brad, too, so we never tried it again." She screwed her mouth up as her face grew serious. "Do you think that's what Luke used on Karina?"

"I'm not sure. He probably used straight ketamine. That's what was in my system when I woke up next to Luke's body this morning."

"No!" She looked genuinely shocked. "And your guy?"

"Cal had it in his system, too. Doctor Smith said we'd been hit with enough to take down an elephant."

My sister rubbed her arms as if to ward off a shiver. "I didn't realize. You could have died. I didn't think--"

"Yeah, it's scary. Someone drugged us and moved us while we were unconscious from one side of town to the other. I'm pretty sure they used four-wheelers and stayed off-road."

"God, Kota. Why didn't you tell me this afternoon? I just thought... I mean, it's bad. Luke was dead, but I didn't--"

"It's okay." I let my sister off the hook. "You know me. It's hard to fall apart when keeping busy."

"That's Mom's motto."

"Yes, it is," Mom said from the door. "Now you girls get your butts down stairs for dinner."

"Coming," Michele said. "We'll be there in a minute." When mom was out of earshot, Michele whispered, "Luke has three four-wheelers, and all of his buddies, Ludlow, Jackson, Madison, and Veronica all have one."

"Thanks," I told her. "I can't believe your leaving just when I decide I might like you."

"Hah! Same." She paused for a moment then said, "Don't tell Mom about..."

I shook my head. "I won't. Promise."

Mom, Dad, and all my younger siblings, including Michele, sat down to a full buffet of food at the formal table in the dining room. Mom had made fried pork chops and gravy, with sides of mash potatoes, corn, green beans with bacon, complete with hot rolls.

"What's the occasion?" I asked.

"The occasion, is that we are all together, and we have our health, a roof over our head, clothes on our back, and the means to have a nice meal," my mom said. "Do we need any other reason?"

"Guess not," I murmured. I took my usual seat, glad there were still a place open for Cal. "Uhm, I hope you don't mind but I invited a friend over for dinner."

My dad looked up from his plate. "Who?"

I didn't even hesitate. "Cal Rivers." While I was uncertain about what would become of my relationship with Cal, I was completely certain that I wanted a relationship. Which meant, I was going to have to include my parents at some point. Granted, my timing could have been better.

"What do you know about him?" my dad asked.

"I know he's kind and protective, and I know he's crazy about me."

Michele guffawed. "Sounds about right to me. He's been

after your twitchy tail for months."

"Michele," Mom admonished. To me, she said, "Does he know he's late for dinner?"

"I invited him after you called us down." It dawned on me that I was being rude to my mom in a way she definitely didn't deserve. "I'm sorry. I'll text him and tell him to pick me up after."

"You're going out tonight?" That threw her more than the surprise dinner guest announcement. "After everything that happened today?"

"The girl is an adult, Ruth," Dad said. But he gave me a wary stare. "You be careful, though. The town's thick with anti-lycanthrope sentiment right now."

"I'll be careful, Dad."

"Don't text him," Mom said. "He can eat with us. Emma, go get another place setting for Dakota's friend."

Emma sighed the sigh of the "put out," but got up to retrieve a plate and silverware from the kitchen.

Lisa looked like she was going to either punch someone or start crying. Thomas and Butch were trading quick jabs in the upper arm when Mom and Dad weren't looking, and Linus, well, Linus was quietly singing the mash potato song. In the past, I'd seen them all as burdens and responsibilities. And, in a way, they always would be. But Linus and Lisa were out of diapers. Emma and Butch were both old enough to drive now, so they could take over some of the chauffeuring of the younger kids. Lisa and Linus were definitely old enough to start taking on more chores.

"I'm moving out," I announced. The whole room turned to me, all of them looking like the proverbial deer in the headlights.

Emma walked in and took one look around and said, "What?"

"Kota is moving out," Linus said unhappily.

Lisa started crying. "I didn't mean it," she said. "I..." She sniffed. "I d-d-didn't mean it. I don't hate you. Please don't move."

"Oh, Lisa." I got up and walked over to her and looped my arm around her. "You can tell me you hate me a thousand times, and I would never believe it. I know you love me. And I love you."

"Then why are you leaving?"

The boys were silent for once, along with the rest of the family, while they waited for me to answer.

"It's time. I have some savings put away for first and last month's rent. I love all of you, but if I stay, things won't change for me. I need my own life. I need you all to rely on me just a little less."

"That werewolf put these ideas in your head," Thomas muttered angrily.

"Dude." I narrowed my gaze on my brother. "Not cool.

First of all, Cal is a lycanthrope, and secondly, he hasn't put any ideas in my head." Well, not the kind of ideas my brother was thinking of anyhow. "I didn't realize just how much I was living my life for you all."

My mother opened her mouth to protest, but I stopped her.

"It's not your fault," I said, addressing her and Dad. "I was always ready to help. Eager even. I was the oldest girl, and I saw how tired Mom was, all the time, with some many of us. I wanted to make her life easier. I wanted it to be easier for both of you, and it made me happy to do it. After a while, though, it had become routine. You both began to expect that I would take up the slack, and I never gave you any reason to think that's not the way I wanted it."

My dad cleared his throat. "It would be unfair for us to let you take all the blame here. You have been the biggest blessing, and if you need to move to have your own life, then you have my blessing."

"Ed!" my mom protested. She paused and took a deep breath. "You don't have to move out. I can expect less from you with you living right here at home. You need breathing room, I'll give it to you."

"It wouldn't work like that, though, would it. Linus would need a lift to practice, Lisa medicine, and we would fall back into the same old habits. And I'm not saying don't ever call me to help out. I'm a part of this family, and I always will be. I just need a little...distance."

"If you want to take a break from the garage," my dad said, "I'll manage. I can hire someone to take your place until one of these knuckleheads take an interest in the shop."

"Don't you dare," I told him. I smoothed down my dress and went to my father. I put my arms around his neck and kissed his cheek. "I love cars. I love trucks. I love getting my fingers knuckle deep in bearing grease. Being a mechanic, running the shop with you, that's the only job I ever want, and there is no way I'm going to let any of these knuckleheads take that away from me."

Dad laughed and patted my arm. "Good, because there's not another mechanic around who has your level of skill." The amount of pride in his voice filled me with warmth.

I went to Mom and put my hand on her shoulders. "It's not like I'm moving away from Peculiar to run off with some integrator."

"Heaven forbid," my mom said.

Michele goggled at me. *Gotcha*, I thought as I gave her a wink.

The doorbell rang, bringing my confession to an end. "I still have to find a place, so it's not like I'm moving out tonight," I told them as I headed to the door. "But I am going out tonight after dinner."

"Fine," Mom said, "but hurry up and let your guest in before the food gets cold."

CHAPTER SEVENTEEN

*C*al whistled when we got into his truck. "Man, you were not exaggerating about your mom's pie. I could die a happy man if that was my last meal."

"As you told her a half-dozen times," I said.

He grinned at me. "Too much?"

"Just enough."

"By the way, is your family always that quiet during dinner?"

I hadn't told Cal about my straight talk with my family, yet. "I think they were all just enjoying good company." I leaned over and gave him a kiss. "I know I was."

Cal started the truck, but before he could put it in gear, something slapped against the window. I stared out, only seeing my reflection in the glass at first, then nearly jumping out of my skin as Lisa's face came into view.

I lowered the window. "You almost made me pee myself!"

"Bobby and I went to check out the fainting goats last night," she blurted. Her hands were shaking as she steadied herself on the door. She had her backpack over her shoulder.

My first impulse was to chastise her for going back to Robyn Smith's farm after she'd been told not to, but something bad must have happened to have her so distraught. The time for recrimination would be later.

I opened the truck door and pulled her inside. She was a little too old to be on my lap, but she climbed up on me anyhow. "Go on, Lisa," I said, keeping my voice soft and soothing. "Tell me what happened."

"The Smith place is next to the Dwyer farm. Bobby and I were going to see if we could get the goats to fall over, but we heard a noise like pig grunting. We saw Bobby's brother Ludlow, carrying something large over his shoulder. Luke was with him. Bobby thought it would be funny if we scared them. Just a little prank is all."

"What time was this?"

She shook her head. "I'm not sure. About ten-thirty maybe. Mom had tucked me in at nine, and I snuck out a little after."

Lord, sneaking out at fourteen. This child was going to be wilder than Michele. "Then what happened."

"There's some cow stalls on the Dwyer place near where

they were standing, so we snuck inside and climbed the walls. And when they drew closer, we jumped out and screamed. Ludlow dropped what he was holding.

She sucked in a sharp breath.

"It was Ronnie Talbert." Lisa closed her eyes tight and shook her head as if trying to shake the memory. "Ronnie, was, she... she wasn't dressed. I could hear her crying, and her voice was slurred."

Cal made a sharp, chuffing sound, but he didn't interject himself into the conversation. I appreciated his ability to not interfere and let me handle it.

Lisa continued, "Ludlow started yelling at Bobby and me, and Luke was yelling at him. Ronnie staggered to her feet, and Luke hit her, right in the face." Lisa put her hand over her mouth as a sob escaped her. "I started yelling at Luke to leave her alone. He jumped at me, but Ludlow stopped Luke from grabbing me. He dropped a packet of white powder and pills." Lisa dug into her backpack and pulled out a small snack-sized sandwich baggy. She handed it to me. "Then Luke and Ludlow were fighting, and Ronnie was staggering toward the fence. Bobby took me by the arm and we ran. He made me swear not to tell. He doesn't want his brother in trouble. But...Ronnie. I don't know if she's okay. And Luke's dead. Is this my fault?"

"No," I told her. "This is not your fault. I wish you'd have told me sooner, or anyone sooner, though. Those drugs might be the lead the police need to find out who killed Luke."

"I'm glad he's dead," Lisa said. While I shared the senti-ment, her conviction made me sad.

"He can't hurt anyone anymore."

"I'm worried he did something bad to Ronnie." Lisa wiped her nose on her sleeve. "I shouldn't have left her out there. I was scared. I thought Luke was going to kill me and Bobby."

Ludlow stepping in didn't make him a good guy, though, I was thankful Lisa had come out of the night safe. Ludlow must have thought he was home free when Lisa didn't come forward. And Ronnie, well, Luke hitting her explained the bruising. I didn't even want to think about what those two guys would have done to her if Lisa and Bobby hadn't shown up. I'd seen the pictures, so I knew it hadn't been the first time they'd made her a victim. I could almost forgive her my swollen ankle and nose.

"I'll take care of this." I put the packet in my purse. "You get back inside before mom starts worrying, and no sneaking out tonight."

Her lip began to quiver. "Bobby is going to hate me."

"This is the kind of secret that can't be kept. When someone is in danger, you have to let someone know."

WE DROVE without speaking for several minutes as we traveled to Taylor's house. Just yesterday, my life had seemed simple. Uncomplicated. Not anymore. I wondered if Ronnie knew the full extent of what had happened to her. What Luke and Ludlow had done and what they planned to do again. Cal held my hand, waiting for me to process what Lisa had told me.

"I'm going to have to tell Mom," I said, breaking the silence between us. "About Lisa, I mean."

"You should," Cal said. "I think she might be suffering from the effects of PTSD. She's going to need someone she can talk to, maybe even outside of the family."

"Like a therapist."

Cal put his blinker light on and turned down Taylor's street. "It helped me after I was shot."

"You saw a counselor?"

"Yeah," he said. "I needed support. I'd never killed anyone before. Not even when I was in Afghanistan. I would defend myself again if I had to, but I still sometimes see O'Brien when I close my eyes. I hope I never have to do it again."

I stared at Cal. His candid retelling of his shooting and resultant killing of a man, and the emotional cost he'd paid, touched me. "I think you might be the bravest, most honest man I've ever met."

"Life's too short to beat around the truth. Nearly dying taught me that lesson."

"I think I understand, at least a little. When I fully realized how vulnerable I'd been last night, what could have happened to me, it had energized me. It made me look at myself and decide what I want to focus on in the future. It made me rethink what I want out of life."

He glanced at me. "And what did you figure out?"

"I am only looking forward from now on." I pivoted my gaze to Cal. "I know what I want, and it's right in front of me."

Cal pulled my hand to his lips and kissed my palm. "That makes me a happy man."

As nice as this was, I couldn't stop thinking about Ludlow and Luke, and the drugs, and my sister, and Ronnie. Cripes. I needed to find Ronnie. She should be seen by the doctor at the very minimum.

"Do you think Eldin will tell us anything?" Cal said as we pulled into the driveway.

"I do. Even if he doesn't, I'm going to tell him about what Lisa saw."

"Ludlow needs to be brought in for questioning," Cal agreed.

"Do you think he killed Luke?"

"Don't you?" Cal put the truck in park and turned off the engine. "It makes sense. If Luke was willing to go at your sister, he might have been willing to go after Bobby as well. So, Ludlow takes out Luke before he can get to his brother."

"It's a strong motive. But why try to frame us?"

"I'd humiliated Luke earlier. We could have just been easy targets of convenience."

"And he hunted us for the pleasure of putting as at the scene." The thought chilled me to my core. He'd had to follow Cal's scent that night. It would have been on Luke and all over me. Lycan's were more pungent than therians. "He watched us going into the woods. He would have had a start point to get our scent, and we would have been easy to track."

Cal nodded. The porch light came on and Taylor opened the door. "You guys going to sit in the drive all night, or are you coming inside?"

"Sakes, he's the spitting image of your angry brother."

"Only his polar opposite," I said. "Taylor is super chill." I waved at my brother. "We better go on in."

Both Taylor and Eldin were in relaxed-fit jeans. Taylor wore a pale green button-down shirt, and Eldin had a black t-shirt that said, "I'm foxy."

I laughed at the pun. "I should start calling before just showing up, huh?" I said. "Are you two going out tonight?"

"There's a new gay bar just outside of Camdenton we want to check out. They are having a Law Enforcement Appreciation night, and police officers get to drink for free," Taylor said.

"I'm going to get lit!" Eldin sang. He nodded to Cal. "Hi. Fancy seeing you here."

"I think someone got an early start," I said to Eldin.

"Oh, just a beer or three. Besides, it's Friday night, I have tomorrow off, and Tay's driving."

"My guy needs to unwind," Taylor said. "From what I hear about this morning, you all do." My brother gave me a hug. "You okay, Kota?"

"I am."

"Mishy called me a few minutes ago. I hear you gave quite the speech at dinner tonight. You're moving out on your own, huh?"

Cal tucked his chin in surprise. "You're doing what?"

I gave Taylor a light punch for spilling the beans. "Okay, so maybe the dead silence at dinner might have been about me declaring my emancipation from my family."

"I think you're very courageous," Taylor said. "It's not easy striking out on your own."

"Was it difficult for you?"

"No, not for me." He jumped away as I tried to punch him again. "Hi," he said to Cal. "I'm Taylor, the good twin."

Cal chuckled. "I met your other half this morning, so I can't say I disagree with you."

"I'm his other half," Eldin pouted.

"You're my better half," Taylor corrected. "Cal's right. Biologically, Tyler is my other half." He stared off as if reliving a fond memory. "He's not a bad guy. He's just...a little stuck. He's never been good at rolling with the flow but he usually gets there." Taylor put his hands in his pockets and went up on his toes. "So, what brings the two of you by?"

For a moment, I let them be happy, because I was about to blow up their night out, and not in a good way.

CHAPTER EIGHTEEN

*S*heriff Taylor had insisted Cal and I come down to the station. I thought we would have gotten a little more quid pro quo from Eldin, but he'd called the sheriff the second he'd heard drugs, date rape, and murder come out of my mouth.

I sat at Tyler's desk, my broody brother glowering at me, while the sheriff had taken Cal into his office and closed the door behind them.

"What do you think they're talking about in there?" I asked.

Tyler ignored me.

The white board wasn't covered now, so I got to see what had been concealed earlier in the day. The columns were in order of type of complaint, address, complainant initials, and the date. So, SD, 900 SW 23, LD, and today's date had to be suspicious death, the Hackenstraw property address, Luke Dwyer. Above it there was another complaint, SA, ??, VT, and it was dated last night. Sexual Assault, maybe, location unknown, and Veronica Talbert. Did this mean she'd reported Luke? But if that had been the case, why wasn't Ludlow already in jail?

"When did Ronnie Talbert come in to file a complaint?" I asked Tyler, who was working the evening shift.

He snarled at me in response. "That's police business."

I snarled back. "Considering our little sister is an eye witness, I'd say it was Thompson family business as well, wouldn't you?"

Tyler grimaced. "Sometimes you are so much like Mom, it's scary."

"I'll take that as a compliment."

He shook his head. "Why didn't you come to me first? Why go to Eldin?"

"I love you, brother, but you can be difficult on a good day. Just look at the way you acted this morning. You went off on Cal without any evidence of wrong doing just because he's different. You judged him in a way that you never would have Luke or even Ludlow, and they are the bad guys here, not Cal."

Tyler groaned. "Fine. I'm an asshole."

"The first step in fixing a problem is admitting you have one." I gave him a fond smile. "Now, tell me when Ronnie came in."

"I took her report. She walked into the station at three this morning and claimed she'd been assaulted, but she couldn't remember by who or where it even took place. She was pretty out of it. I called Willy, because she's trained with the sexual assault kit, something she'd volunteered to learn last year. We had one report a couple months ago, well, I can't talk about the case, but it was similar to Ronnie's. The girl didn't remember much of the night, and when it came down to it, she refused to name her attacker."

I wondered if it had been Karina Wells. Had she mustered enough resolve to report the attack? Only to lose courage at the last minute. Had she blamed herself? If she had gone through with her complaint, would it have stopped Luke? Would she have been believed? It didn't matter. She was a victim, and I wouldn't make her complicit for being afraid to come forward.

"And Ronnie?"

"She left after the preliminary questions. The fact that she couldn't remember what had happened to her upset her. Willy tried to get her to go see the doctor, but Ronnie refused. We can't force victims to consent."

"Of course," I said. Now that Tyler was talking to me, I nodded toward the sheriff's office again. "What do you think the sheriff wants with Cal?"

"To offer him a job."

"You're kidding."

Tyler curled his lip at me. "Do I look like I'm kidding?"

"Almost never," I said.

"Ha ha." He rolled his eyes. "With the lycanthropes in town, and Cal's background in law enforcement, the sheriff thinks he could help diffuse some of the current tension in town. Since the Corman's have been sponsoring Cal and his Brother, Willy vouched for him with the Tri-State Council, and they have agreed it's worth giving Cal a shot."

"And you?" I asked. "Are you willing to give him a shot?"

"I don't have anything against the lycans," he said. "I was worried about you, and I reacted badly."

"You sure did." I cracked a small smile at him. "I forgive you."

"I'm so glad," he said with dramatic sarcasm. But I could tell he was relieved.

Cal and the sheriff finally came out of the office. "Cal is officially a sheriff's deputy," he said. "But you're not, Dakota. So, I'll ask you to go home and stay there until we can find Davis and bring him in."

I wanted to argue, but how in the world could I make a case that didn't make me sound like I just didn't want to be left out of the chase. If Ludlow was responsible for our predicament and Luke's death, I wanted to see him brought to justice.

I huffed, feeling peevish. "Fine." I gestured to them. "Go get him. I'll get myself home."

My phone rang. Mom came up on the screen. I picked up. "Hey, Mom. What's up?"

"Do you know where your sister is?"

Great, Michele just couldn't stay out of trouble. Not even one night. "Have you called her?"

"And called her and called her." There was an edge of fear and panic in her voice.

"I'll try her. Michele has a boyfriend. Brad Connors. She's probably out with him."

"Michele is here with me," Mom said. "Lisa is the one missing. I've called Bobby Davis's mom, and he's missing, too. Where would she go? Why would she just take off with everything going on? She's acting so out of character. I'm about to lose my flippin' mind!"

Tyler had been standing close enough to me to hear the entire conversation. "I'll start calling everyone to start forming search parties."

"What's happening," Sheriff Taylor asked.

"Mom says, Lisa's missing. So is Bobby Davis." I leaned against a nearby desk, suddenly light-headed. "What if Ludlow has them?"

Tyler took my phone. Calmly, he instructed my mother to

put the rest of our younger siblings on lockdown, and for her and dad to come to the station.

"This is my fault," I said. I felt the blood rush from my limbs. "I should have told Mom and Dad the minute Lisa confessed to me about what had happened. I could have kept her safe."

Cal put his arm around me as my knees buckled. He held me up. "This isn't your fault, Dakota," he said. "This isn't your fault."

———

MOM'S BEST FRIENDS, Willy, Chavvah, and Sunny surrounded her, keeping her occupied as Babel Trimmel, Doc Smith, Brady Corman, and Roger Messer worked with Sheriff Taylor to call all the able-bodied men and women in town who were willing to volunteer to find the missing teens. Jo Jo had come in with Dale and Brady, and Etta had come in with her dad and Chav to help out. The last big search had taken place when Jo Jo and my sister Michele had gone missing during the Tri-State Council Jubilee. They had been tied up and left in the woods by two serial killing brothers, who had used our search for them as a distraction, so they could claim their real target, which had been Chavvah.

I prayed we would find Lisa and Bobby safe, the same way we'd found Jo Jo and Michele safe.

"I'm joining the search party," I told Cal. "And heaven help any of you if you try to stop me."

"You can ride with me," he said with no hesitation. "I was going to suggest it anyhow."

"Does anyone know where Ludlow is? Do you really think he'd hurt his brother? Especially if he went through all the trouble to kill Luke to protect him."

"We don't know that for certain, so until we do, we have to assume he's capable of anything. The sooner we find Lisa and the boy, the better."

"Does this mean you don't know where Ludlow is?"

"The sheriff says Mrs. Davis hasn't seen him, and he isn't at any of his usual haunts."

I nodded. It had only been forty minutes since Mom had called me, but it had felt like forty hours. Every minute not searching for Lisa felt like wasted time.

"We should be out there now," I said.

"A grid search is the most effective. That way we aren't looking in the same spots over and over. Your mom brought over some of Lisa's clothing, and Roberta Davis is bringing in some of Bobby's. Since lycanthropes have a keener sense of smell, there will be a few of us in each group."

"Good. We need all the advantage we can get."

"Okay, team leaders," Sheriff Taylor announced. "We have some three-hundred volunteers out on the courthouse lawn already divided up into twenty groups by Deputy Farraday and Deputy Connelly."

I teared up at the sheer number of people ready to help. Small towns had their problems, especially when it came to distrust of outsiders, but moments like this, the way the community pulled together to support each other, that's what made places like Peculiar great.

The sheriff continued his instructions. "As soon as Mrs. Davis comes in with some of Bobby's clothing, we will make sure that each group has a big enough sample to recognize Lisa or Bobby's scent. Deputy Boden will coordinate things here at the station as our home base. Any information you find or receive should be disseminated directly through her and no one else. Got it?"

There was a murmur of agreement in the room.

Roberta Davis showed up a few minutes later, and the hunt was on.

CHAPTER NINETEEN

*D*ad was in our group, along with Taylor, Etta, Jo Jo, Mark Smart, and twelve others. We'd been given the Dwyer farm and Robyn Smith's property to search, as a possible location. The overcast sky threatening rain, darkened the pastures, as intermittent zaps of lightning would temporarily blind us. Since Missouri weather changed minute by minute, I prayed the rain would hold off a little longer. A heavy downpour would make tracking Lisa's scent impossible.

Each team was given a two-way radio on a lanyard to wear around their necks when shifted. Therianthropes began to disrobe, everyone shifting into their animal forms, then one by one sniffing Lisa and Barry's clothing. Some of us had better olfactory senses than others, but I knew Cal had the best chance of catching their trail before anyone else. I put the radio around my neck, before shifting. My deer appeared next to Cal's wolf, and I flitted my ears back and forth when he nuzzled me, a reassuring gesture, with his head.

Cal had carefully laid out the plan where each team of two would search on the property. The Dwyer property had a lot of pasture, but some dense woods, while Robyn Smith's place was just the opposite. She had a lot of woods, and a small three-acre area of pasture. I had wanted to go there, because I was holding out hope that Lisa had simply ran away to see the goats again. But since Cal was my partner, we needed to be where the best cross-breeze could point us in the right direction, not just the direction I hoped we'd find them in. So, we did a slow walk along the fence line between the properties. Cal's nose was to the ground, mine was to the air.

The dampness in the air clung to my nostrils as I inhaled deeply, keeping my ears attuned to our surroundings. Cal's nose might be better, but I had super hearing, thanks to my big doe ears. However, after nearly three hours of searching, all I could smell and hear were the other searchers and those damn fainting goats. I was worried we were nowhere near the right area. I began to snort and paw at the ground in frustration. My deer let out a loud snort that ended in a wheeze. Cal's wolf crouched as he transformed back into human. I followed suit.

"This is stupid. They're not here. Where would he take them?"

Cal rubbed my arms as fear made me shiver.

"I thought for sure Lisa would be here. I hoped--"

"We won't give up, Dakota," Cal promised. "We'll find your sister and Bobby, and we will bring them home. Heck, they might already be home if one of the other teams have found them already."

"Willy would have called," I said. I knew I sounded defeated, but I couldn't stop blaming myself. "Lisa has to be okay. She has to be safe."

"Let's keep looking. We have about a mile of fence line left. Let's get it done, then we will pick a side and head in that direction. Grid searches are slow and tedious, but they work. You have to trust the process."

I nodded. "Okay." I touched the radio, willing it to come to life. When it didn't, I went back to four legs and a tail.

Then I froze at a distant sound. I curled my ear in the direction of the foreign noise. It was a *tin-tin tin-tin*, dull and patterned. Not a nature made sound. Too deliberate.

Cal hadn't shifted back into a wolf, yet. "What do you hear?" I twitched my tail and glanced in the direction of the Smith homestead. Robyn was in one of the search parties somewhere near Mark Smart's property. No one had been allowed to search their own place, because it could muddy the scent pool. *Tin-tin tin-tin*. There it was again. Definitely not the goats. My heart began to beat wildly in my chest. I pointed with my head in the direction of Robyn's farmhouse and barn. The noise was coming from that direction.

"Switch back," Cal said, "and tell me what you're hearing."

I couldn't waste any more time. Lisa was in danger. Danger I could have prevented. I leaped away from Cal, then I ran, kicking off hard with my back legs until I picked up full speed. I had the faintest thought that I should wait for Cal, but an overriding sense of panic for my sister kept me running headlong toward her rescue. Cal would catch up, I rationalized. He knew my scent. He could follow me anywhere.

I jumped fallen trees, small brooks, one good-sized ditch, and a large rock as I made my way through the densely-wooded property. When I could see the barn, I slowed to a complete stop and listened for the noise. When I didn't hear anything, I walked closer to the exposed pasture surrounding the farm. A baleful howl of a wolf cut through the trees, and I heard the thud of several goats as they collapsed from fear.

Tin-tin. There it was again! I ran toward the barn. Inside, the goats had been put up in stalls with wooden doors that lined one side of the barn. The ones that hadn't fainted, shuffled nervously. *Tin-tin*. Hope surged through me as I scanned the room. The noise was coming from the end stall.

I bleated triumphantly as I rushed to the door, shifted into my human form, and threw it open. "Lisa!" Inside, Ludlow Davis, covered in goat blood, and holding a knife in one hand and a pistol in the other, tapped the blade and the barrel. *Tin-tin*.

He smiled at me as he turned the gun in my direction.

"I've been waiting for someone to party with. I'm so glad it's you."

"Where's my sister?" I asked. "What have you done with her?"

"Come in here and close the door." He waved the gun at me to emphasize his demand. "You are a rotten bitch, you know that." He threw bailing twine at me. "Tie your ankles. That way if you shift on me, you can't run away." Ludlow's red hair was matted with straw as if he'd been living in the barn for weeks. His pupils were constricted to tiny dots, which meant his normal night vision was crap right now.

He was high on his own junk.

I tied my ankles, my right ankle really sore after running and jumping and doing everything the doc told me not to do.

Ludlow was too stoned to be scared, so I tried to unnerve him. "You know you're being tracked. The sheriff has half the town out looking for you. I'm not the only one searching for Lisa and Bobby."

The mention of his brother's name did the trick. "Bobby?"

"Yes. Your mother is really worried. She gave us some of Bobby's clothes to track him."

Ludlow shook his head. "No, no, no. This is Luke's fault. All his fault. I didn't do it. Any of it."

"That's right," I said. "It's not your fault. I bet killing Luke was an accident. Trying to pin his death on the werewolves was self-preservation, right? I get it."

"You know I'm not as dumb as most people think I am," he said. He pulled out a bag of powder, he scooped a little out with his knife and snorted it off the edge. He did it again and held the point of the knife out in my direction. "Your turn," he said.

"Uhm, no thanks." I tried to take a step back and stumbled against the door.

"Do it or I'll cut you?" Ludlow said. "I'll make you bleed."

"Ludlow," I heard Cal say. "Let Dakota go. You don't want to hurt her."

"He has a gun!" I warned him.

"Shut up, wolf. You don't know what I want," my captor scoffed. "But you're right. I don't want to hurt her. I want to make her feel good. But if you so much as rattle the stall door, I swear, I will gut her like I gutted the goat." I shuddered as he shoved the knife into the powder again and put it in front of my face. "Now snort this before I decide to dump the whole bag down your throat."

"Don't do this," Cal said. I could hear the agony in his tone. "I swear if you hurt her I will kill you."

"Violence is not the answer," Ludlow said. "That's what Mom always says. But dad liked to knock us around, so while it wasn't the answer she wanted, it was an answer all the same." He laughed. "Come on, Bambi. Take a bump. It will free your mind."

I leaned forward, my nose perilously close to the blade, while keeping a sharp eye on the gun. "Cal," I said. "Are you there?"

"Yeah, Dakota. I'm here. I'm right here."

"I'm falling in love with you," I told him. "I just want you to know...just in case."

"You're getting out of here, Dakota. We both are. Just..."

"Shut the hell up! Gah. I can't take all the pathetic love stuff. I want to party." He thrust the knife at me, and it scratched my cheek. The drug powder burned in the wound before it started to go numb.

He shook the pistol at me. "Just in case you get the idea that I won't shoot you." *Blam*! The gun went off, and I cried out when the hot bullet grazed my left thigh.

A roar that shook the rafters drove me to my knees as Cal's half-form towered above the stall door.

"I'm okay!" I warned him. But it was too late, because Ludlow pointed the gun at Cal and he pulled the trigger again. *Blam*! I screamed as Cal went down. The noise startled Ludlow enough to stagger him. I'd never done a partial transformation, but I willed my arms and shoulders to take on my powerful doe form, and when my thick muscles had appeared, and my hands became hard hooves, I reared back and began to pummel Ludlow about the face, neck, and chest. One of my blows knocked the gun away, and he dropped the knife trying to defend himself against my kicks. I screamed my rage, and only when he was on the ground and no longer moving did I stop.

"Cal!" I shouted as I flung the stall door open.

He had had a wound in his upper right arm, but he was sitting up, much to my relief. "Are you okay?" he asked.

"I'm fine. I'm more than fine." I dropped down beside him. "You scared the crap out of me."

My radio flared. "Lisa and Bobby have been found. All teams come back to base."

I breathed a heavy sigh of relief.

Cal looked past me to Ludlow's still body. "Did you kill him?"

"I don't think so. But I beat his head in pretty good, so I'm not sure what kind of life he'll have."

Cal pressed his palm to my cheek. "You scared the crap out of me. No more running into danger, okay?"

I nodded. "I scared myself."

"And, about what you said...I'm not falling--"

"It's okay if you don't feel the same way," I told him. "I know I can't be your one. Your real mate, but I'll take what I can get. I want to be with you as long as you'll have me."

Cal's brow crinkled. "What are you talking about with this 'the one' stuff?"

"It's okay. Etta told me about you all. That lycanthropes can only mate with lycanthropes, and one day you will find that special someone. But I figure as long as I keep you here and away from any hot wolves you haven't already met..."

"First, Etta was raised by a puritanical maniac who believes the only way lycanthropes can stay strong is by not contaminating our blood lines with other species. So he told her that bullshit to keep her from dating outside of town. That kind of thinking made us sterile for years. And I think Chavvah Smith is proof that his theory is bunk. She is part coyote, part wolf. Could that happen if lycans couldn't mate with therians?"

"Okay, I feel dumb."

He nodded. "Etta should feel dumb. Second, I'm not falling in love with you, because I'm already in love with you, so I'm in for however long you want me. The rest of my life would do me just fine."

"Deal," I said. The sound of voices from our group nearing the barn, told me that most of them had shifted back to human. They must have heard the shots.

"We're okay!" I yelled. I grabbed the radio. "This is Dakota Thompson. We have Ludlow Davis captured in Robyn Smith's barn."

A low moan from Ludlow drew our attention.

"Tell Doc Smith he's going to need medical attention."

Cal grinned at me. "Such a bad ass."

"I'm your bad ass," I said then grimaced. "I really do need to work on my sexy talk."

"You do just fine," Cal said. "Just fine."

CHAPTER TWENTY

I stretched out in bed after sleeping the sleep of the dead. Twelve hours straight. As stiff and sore as I was, I doubted I'd moved even an inch.

Lisa and Bobby, it had turned out, had not been kidnapped by drugged out Ludlow. Apparently, Bobby had ran away from home, called Lisa, and begged her to come with him. Since she is fourteen, hormonal, and in love, she said, yes. Mom has grounded her until she's old enough to vote. She says they will renegotiate the terms of the grounding at that time. After a cursory exam, Doc said that Ludlow would eventually recover to stand trial for Luke's death and for the drugs.

After everyone returned home, Cal dropped me off at home. I couldn't tossed and turned in bed before I grabbed a change of clothes and drove straight to Jo Jo's. Best decision ever.

And I slept with him.

WHO LET THE WOLVES OUT?

You know, actual sleep.

"You snore," Cal said, snuggling up behind me.

I rolled over to face him. "Do not."

"How do you know? You can't hear yourself when you're sleeping."

"Is snoring a deal breaker?"

"Nope," he said. He wrapped his arms around me, and I laid my head on his chest. "Not a deal breaker."

"Then, fine, I snore." I kissed his chest. The hair tickled my lips. "You are hot," I said.

"Thank you," he replied.

"I mean like heat hot. My back is all sweaty from you being pressed up against me during the night."

Cal chuckled. "Is that a deal breaker?"

I snorted. "Not hardly."

I'd put on one of Cal's t-shirts to sleep in, and he was in nothing but his boxer briefs. These ones had a dancing rooster on them, and they said, my cock knows all the right moves. I laughed with gusto. "Sunny said I'd have dancing chickens in my future." I gave him a sly wink. "But what I want to know, is if it's true?" I asked, snapping the band of his underwear. "Does your cock have all the right moves?"

He pulled me up into his arms and kissed me in a way that

made my eyelashes curl. "I can tell you," he said. "Or I can show you."

"Oh, I'm all for a personal demonstration." I grinned at him. "You know, a try before you buy situation."

"Is that a challenge?"

I giggled. "Possibly."

He rolled over on top of me, then went up on his knees between my thighs. He bent over and slid the t-shirt up my torso. He kissed my inner thigh, and I squirmed. A demanding ache pulsed at my core, and I soaked my panties.

Cal licked them and growled. Oh, the big, bad wolf fantasies flashed before my eyes as I knew, he was about to feast. He slid my underwear down my legs and off my feet then used his hands to spread my thighs. He stroked a finger over my throbbing clit.

"Oh, God," I moaned. He slid the finger inside me, and I began to shake. "This is going to go quick," I warned him.

He chuckled, and it got me in all my low places. His eyes were half-lidded as he lay down between my knees and licked the slit of me.

"Yep, yep," I said, my voice strained.

He laughed then.

"It's not funny," I said.

"No," he said. "It's sexy as hell." He curled his tongue around my motherload and sucked it between his teeth.

"That's it!" I exploded around his finger as the orgasm rocked me hard. Cal kept with me, stroking and licking until I finally stopped shuddering. I let out a stuttered sigh. "Okay," I teased. "I'm good."

"Yes, you are." Cal moved up my body, and somewhere along the line, he'd managed to lose the dancing cock undies. "Now, I'm going to show you just how good I am." He slid inside me, his thick girth stretching me wide. I groaned at the weighted feel of him as he began to move with me. I swallowed, my throat dry from moaning my pleasure with his every thrust. After a few minutes, the burn of desire began to build again as our bodies danced like old lovers. I wrapped my legs around his waist, and he began to thrust harder.

"Oh, God, Dakota. Yes. You feel so good," he said. "So good." His eyes rolled back a little on an up thrust. "So tight. Damn."

I rocked against him, loving the friction of his body against me as he made me his completely. The well filled once again, threatening to spill at any moment. "Oh, oh," I said. "I'm-- Ah!" I quaked, grasping and pulling at him as my lower body detonated.

"Christ," Cal muttered then threw his head back as he came so hard I felt him pulsing inside me. By the time we were finished, we were both quivering bodies of used up, but in an awesome way, flesh. When he softened enough to pull out, he dropped beside me on to the bed, a fine layer of sweat on his skin. "Jesus, woman. You're incredible."

"You can keep the underwear I told him. You were not oversold. Your dancing cock has all the right moves."

"You are still not alone in the house," Jo Jo yelled from the hallway.

Cal and I stared at each other then laughed. Then we rested, then we made love again. And when Jo Jo complained again, we laughed again. And we repeated the activity over and over, with minor food and pee breaks until the next day.

I HATED GETTING out of bed on Sunday. Worse, I hated that I'd been roped into singing at Luke Dwyer's memorial service. Mom had called to remind me bright an early. Cal promised to show up for moral support. Thank heavens, because I wasn't sure I would make it through the afternoon without him.

The sky was overcast as I drove down the road toward town. I could not stop thinking about Cal. I'd never had anyone make me feel the way he did. I didn't have to act with Cal. I was a total dork, and he liked that about me. Heck, he loved that about me.

I was grinning like a fool when my truck suddenly lurched forward, sputtered, popped, and I managed to get it off to the side of the road before it came to an abrupt halt. *Nooooo*! I tried turning it over and was rewarded with a *clunk-clunk*.

"Son-of-a-biscuit eater." I texted Cal. *Truck dead. No resurrection imminent. Come pick me up.*

I waited for his response, but when nothing happened, I pulled up my contacts to phone mom. As luck would have it, though, Mrs. Dwyer's sedan drove up behind me.

Jack Trevors was driving her again. He got out and walked up to my door. "Do you need help?"

"My truck finally bit the dust."

He gave me a lopsided smile. "You're a mechanic, right?"

"Yeah, yeah," I said. "I always thought I'd have time to get around to it, but I guess not."

"Why don't you ride in with us? I can drop you off at your house, and Mary Ann would appreciate the company. She's had a few really difficult days. Yesterday, the sheriff told her about Luke and, well, you know. I'm really worried about her."

I didn't want to ride with Mary Ann, but I remembered Mom's words. The woman had lost her only child, and that loss runs deeper than all others. So, I nodded. "Sure. I'd appreciate it." I grabbed my phone and my purse, put the hazard lights on, before leaving my truck.

I climbed in the back seat of the car with Mrs. Dwyer. She wore all black, including a black hat with matching lace to cover her eyes. "Hi, ma'am. Thank you for offering me a lift."

"Of course, dear." She dabbed at her eyes with a tissue. "I'm not ready for today."

"Me either." I meant the singing of course, but I let her read into it whatever gave her comfort. All the time I had dated Luke, I never really saw Jack Trevors with the family, so it kind of surprised me that he was driving her around. I wonder if they'd started expecting more from Jack when they gave him a place to live. I knew first-hand how expectations could lead you down a path you didn't want to take.

"Hey, Jack. How did you like your apartment there on the lake front? I'm looking for a place, and I heard they were nice."

"Good. A little expensive, but there is the view."

Mrs. Dwyer clasped her hands and picked at her nail. The new polish from Friday was now chipped and damaged. A casualty of stress and grief.

"I can't even imagine what you're going through," I said. "Losing your only child is such a terrible thing."

From the driver seat, Jack said, "It'll all be over soon."

My blood went cold, and I felt as if death passed through me. "What did you say?"

"It'll all be over..." He peered at me through the rearview mirror, his expression one of a man caught by his own dumb-assery. "Soon." Jack was the man who'd shot me with the tranquilizer dart. He'd drugged me and had tried to frame Cal and me for Luke's death. But why? Why go through all that trouble? He wasn't even on anyone's radar.

My phone buzzed. *Just out of shower. Coming to get you*, he texted. *Stay put.*

Mrs. Dwyer leaned over to look at my text. "Is that your new friend?" she asked.

I nodded. With Luke's mom staring over my shoulder, I worried if I just came out with, hey, I'm trapped in a car with a murderer, Mrs. Dwyer would lose it and put us both at greater risk. Instead, I tried to let Cal know what was going on without putting us in more danger.

I typed as fast as my fingers would allow. *Mrs. D and Jack T picked me up on the road. Taking me to town. Jack says, it will all be over soon.*

Wavy dots .... More wavy dots ... *Meet you in town. If I can't find you, I'll see you on the full moon.*

CHAPTER TWENTY-ONE

"*S*he knows," Jack said.

"Shut up, Jack," Mrs. Dwyer said.

"I'm telling you, she knows."

"Let me think," she said.

I tried to get off another text, but the older deer shifter slapped my phone from my hand. It landed in the floor. When I tried to pick it up, Jack slammed on the breaks, skidding on the road and throwing me into the back of the seat.

Mrs. Dwyer looked concerned. Apologetic even, but she wasn't trying to help me.

Oh, heck, no. "Jack killed your son."

"How do you know?"

"Because the last thing I remember was him telling me it

would all be over soon. Why are you protecting him?" I made a grab for the door handle, but the locked engaged.

"Child safety locks," Jack said. He had a gun pointed at me now. "Don't move."

"Her wolf is on the way, Jack." Mrs. Dwyer said. "We need to move."

"I think we should kill her," he said.

"I guess it's a good thing I don't pay you to think!" Mrs. Dwyer screeched. She took a deep breath, reached into her hand bag, and pulled out a syringe.

"What is that?" I scooted toward the door. I did not want to be tranquilized again.

"It's pentobarbital, enough to kill an adult therianthrope." She stared at the clear liquid with a longing I didn't understand.

"You were always planning to kill me?" I asked.

"Oh, child. This was for me, not you. It would have been my final act after burying my youngest son."

Youngest? "Luke was an only child."

"No," she said. "I was married before I met Jonathan. I used to be an integrator, you know."

"Yes. Mom told me the story of when you first moved to town. You became fast friends."

"Your mom is a special woman. That's why this is so

difficult."

"Why did Jack kill Luke? Why are you helping him?"

"I didn't kill the spoiled brat," Jack said. "I kept him from destroying himself as long as I could. I protected him. Until I couldn't." Jack stared at Mrs. Dwyer. "That's what older brother's do."

I blinked, trying to process what he was saying. "But you're... you're not a deer?"

"My dad was a coyote. I got my beast from him. He told me my mother died, but I found out the truth three years ago when he got cancer. He confessed that she was alive, and he told me where she lived. When the Tri-State Council had their meeting here, I used it as an excuse to get to know her. So, she could know me."

"I know more about both my sons than a mother should ever know," Mrs. Dwyer said. She sounded exhausted. "One is a rapist. The other is a sniveling man barely able to take care of himself, let alone a simple thing like, framing a wolf for Luke's death." She shook her head. "You just had to put Dakota at the scene. After I told you I didn't want her involved."

"You killed him," Jack said. "I just covered it up."

"Poorly," Mrs. Dwyer admitted.

Oh. My. God. I felt like I was in the middle of a made for TV drama. "I know you loved Luke. I know you're grieving. That's real. So why did you kill him?"

"I've already said. I found recordings." She shuddered. "He recorded his awful acts against those women. I can't forgive myself for bringing such a monster into the world. Even so, I hadn't meant to. I'd just been so angry. I lashed out." She held her hand out and each one of her nails elongated and thickened like talons, only they were hard like hooves. I'd heard of people controlling aspects of their shift, but this was next level. She examined her hands. "I cut his jugular. He bled out in minutes." She blinked at me. "I'm sorry we got you involved in this Dakota. I've always liked you, but I think Jack's right. I can't let you live. I couldn't save one son, but I can save the other." She popped the plastic cap off the needle of the syringe. "I'll find peace another way."

I had my hand behind my back, focused on turning it into a hoof. Jack had the gun on me, and Mrs. Dwyer had the syringe of death, and all I had was a strong will to live. I hoped it was enough.

"What about Mr. Dwyer? Does he know about Luke? Jack?"

"He knows about Luke now. It's all over town. He refuses to see our son buried. As to Jack, yes, I told him he's my son. He'll have to deal with it. He's the only child we have left, and when I'm gone, Jack will take my place in the family business."

"Mom," Jack said, his attention completely focused on his mother.

I used the opportunity to hit the tempered glass near the

edge with my hoof. It shattered with a loud popping sound. Jack swung his weapon around, but I lunged out the window before he could get it trained on me.

And I ran. A shot rang out, and Mrs. Dwyer was right behind me, yelling at Jack to drive down the road and park. She was super nimble and quick. Quicker than me. Crap. Crap.

I shed my clothes as I high stepped into the woods and soon as my pants were off, I shifted. My panties were a little tight over my tail, and my bra stretched across my barrel chest, but Mrs. Dwyer would have caught up to me if I had taken the time to remove them. I picked up speed as I scented another deer coming up on me fast. I pushed hard with my back legs, pivoting over and past obstacles. Cal would meet me in my place in the Hacken-straw woods. At least I hoped that's what he'd meant when he said he'd meet me at the full moon. I just had to get there.

OVERHEATED, lathered, and panting hard, my deer was exhausted by the time I reached the Hackenstraw prop-erty. I couldn't stop, though. Mrs. Dwyer looked like she could go several more rounds.

I was close now, less than a mile to my little clearing, where I knew Cal would be waiting for me. I just had to run, but my legs, they were so fatigued it felt like I was running through mud with sandbags attached. And my ankle had started to really ache at the stress I had put on it. I began to trot, because it was all I could manage.

That's when the flying deer woman tackled me in a spectacular leap.

"Ayeee!" The noise ripped from me as I tumble to the ground, my legs buckling beneath me. I rolled, my neck twisting at an awkward angle.

My deer was getting pummeled, I had to shift back to have a fighting chance. So, I made myself Dakota. I grabbed at Mrs. Dwyer's wrists to keep her claw-hooves from cutting me up. "Stop," I screamed. Tears were leaking down the side of my face. "Mary Ann, please stop!"

She blinked down at me, her half-human half-deer face gazing at me as if really seeing me. Her fur receded, and she looked mostly human again.

"I don't want to do this," she said. "But I have to. For Jack's sake."

"Cal knows. He'll tell people. Killing me won't save either of you," I told her. "You'll just do the same thing to my mom that has happened to you. You'll turn her into a mother who didn't die before her child. You can't want that for her. You can't want that for your friend."

Her hot tears dripped down on my skin and joined my own. "It's all muddy now." she had me pinned with one monstrous hand while she held out the other. Slowly, it became human again, and where there had been a thick

225

line of keratin, now lay the syringe. "You deserve a peaceful death. I don't," she said. "But you do. I'm sorry." She held up the syringe and plunged it into her neck. "You shouldn't have to watch this. Tell your mother... tell her..."

"Dakota!" Cal shouted.

"Over here," I called back. I eased Mrs. Dwyer aside. I stared at her as she took her last breath and the life left her eyes. And then, I cried.

"It's okay," Cal said, holding me tight. "You're safe."

"Jack," I said.

"We got him. Eldin is taking him to the station."

Tyler, Willy, and the sheriff came running out of the woods toward us, my brother's face so full of worry and dread. Cal stripped his shirt off and put it over my head. My legs were so dead, he had to carry me to the road.

"Why pick a place so far away?" I asked him as he eased me into his truck.

"Your text shook me. It was the only place I could think of quickly."

"You found me, though." I cupped his face. "My hero."

"Face it. You were your own hero. But I'm willing to take the credit if the job comes with perks."

"Like dancing chickens."

"Exactly, like dancing chickens."

EPILOGUE

*O*ne month later...

"You can put those boxes back in the spare bedroom. And the rest of you grab furniture and start hauling it up." My whole family had come out to help me move. The twins were carrying a sofa up to the third-floor apartment I'd rented a few days earlier.

The trial for Jack Trevor and Ludlow Davis hadn't taken but a few weeks. Doctor Smith's autopsy confirmed that Luke had died from exsanguination due to a neck injury. Jack had tried to make it look like a lycan attack by turning into his coyote and mauling Luke to cover the actual wound. Which meant, there was enough evidence against them both to warrant the Tri-Council to send one of their executioners to Peculiar. When I asked about how Mary Ann could master her half-form so completely, Mom told me it took more practice than she ever wanted to do. A lifetime of training. I didn't watch the trials or the conclusions. I wondered how different things would have turned out if Mary Ann Dwyer had just turned herself in after she'd killed Luke. She'd taken both their lives that night, it just took a while longer for Jack to die.

Willy started a counseling group for Luke's victims. Two of the girls hadn't remembered anything about the night, but they had known something bad had happened to them. I just hoped his death gave them the smallest amount of satisfaction.

For me, I was finally moving out on my own. Well, sort of.

Cal put his arms around me. "It's a nice view," he said.

"The lake is beautiful."

He kissed my neck, a low growl in his voice. "I'm not talking about the lake."

I laughed as he slid his hands over my stomach.

"Are we going to tell them?"

"Tell them what?" I asked.

"That you're going to marry me."

"You haven't asked me, yet," I said.

"Woman, I put a baby up in you, how much more of a proposal do you need."

I snorted so loud that my family all turned to look at me. I was only weeks along and not showing. But with theri-anthrope and lycanthrope pregnancies, it would only take another three or four weeks before I looked like I'd swallowed a melon.

"Are you two going to stand around or are you going to help?" Tyler asked.

I ignored my brother and said to Cal. "When you're serious, mister, you will put a ring on it."

Music started playing in the parking lot. I tried to see where it was coming from. "Did someone leave their car stereo on?" Suddenly, Eldin Farraday stepped out into the open. And... he started dancing to "Having My Baby" by Paul Anka. Then Taylor, who was on the steps, started dancing, too. Soon, the parking lot and the stairwell were filling up with our friends, and everyone was dancing and singing. Then Cal let go of me as he belted out the final lyrics as he went down on one knee.

I felt such an intense surge of happiness swell inside me, I thought it might cripple me. He held out a box and flipped it open when the music stopped. Inside was a gold band set with an emerald cut diamond with two sapphires on either side.

"Dakota Augusta Thompson, you're the woman I love, and I want to marry you and have as many babies as you want."

"How about nine," I told him.

He grinned. "Let's make it an even dozen."

"Deal." I held out my hand.

"Is that a yes?"

"Yes, Callum David Rivers, I will marry you."

He put the ring on my finger and kissed me until my toes curled, then shouted, "She said, yes!" to the cheering crowd of our loved ones.

The End

GONE WITH THE MINION - CHAPTER 1

Madder Than Hell Book 1

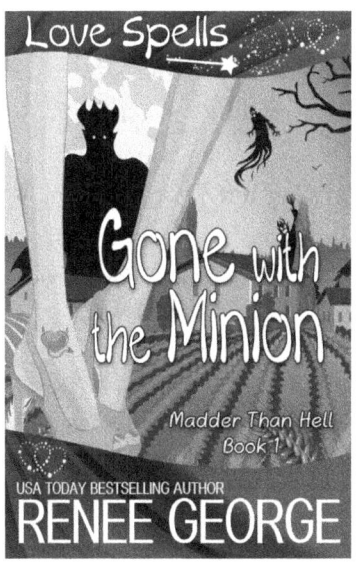

How do you save your family when they're about to lose the literal farm? You make a deal with a demon, of course. And then you spend the next one

hundred and forty-nine years making him sorry he forced you to sign in blood on the dotted line.

To save her family, Southern Belle Olivia "Liv" Madder made a bargain with a demon lord and ever since, she's been haunted...by her three dead sisters, and her own guilty conscience. Every decade, since the deal, Liv has had to find a human willing to bargain their soul with Moloch. If she fails, even once, he'll not only drag her to Hell, but he'll take her sisters, too. It doesn't mean she can't make Lord Jerkface miserable in the process by removing his lesser demons from the Earthly plane.

When her latest contracted soul dies before the bargain is sealed, she has less than four days to find another soul or her own agreement will be broken. But Moloch offers her a get-out-of-Hell-free card: steal an old book once owned by paranormal researcher David Jensen. The same David Jensen she fell in love with sixty years ago but left to protect him and his family. Then Moloch drops the biggest bombshell: David has died.

Heartbroken and feeling she has no choice, Liv makes the trip to Sanctum, Missouri only to find David's grandson has the book. Worse, he's keeping a mysterious family secret that threatens Moloch, Liv, and her three sisters. What's a minion to do when her world falls apart? Get Madder than Hell and kick some demon butt.

Available at All Your Favorite eTailers

Chapter One

It took me two seconds to spot my mark and about half that time for him to spot me. He was on the move. Right out the opened French doors. I could see he was headed toward the garden. Why, oh, why did they always run? I shoved my way through the crowd of monkey suits and silk chiffons with as much grace as I could muster. Not an easy feat considering I was stuffed into the ill-fitting, scarlet-red, mermaid-cut, satin dress I'd...um, borrowed from the unconscious woman in the coat room. A frock more billowy and less mermaid-y would've been a better choice for running, but I'd picked this one because it matched my red stiletto pumps and my patent-leather clutch with its removable silver chain. The little purse hung off my shoulder and slapped against my thigh as I wiggled through the crowd.

I finally made it outside. Freshly blossomed lilacs burst out from the multitude of bushes like tufts of purple cotton candy and sweetened the humid air. I looked over my shoulder and saw that no one noticed, or more likely, cared that I was chasing the party's host into the lavish garden.

The three-story mansion was overly ostentatious, even for Jefferson City, the capital of Missouri. The monstrosity, with its marble columns and wrought-iron balconies, reminded me of the plantation a few miles from my father's modest farm in Georgia, where I'd been born and raised. In other words, the place stuck out like a bedazzled T-shirt at a Sunday morning church service. The owner of the mansion, Carmine Hennessy, was a lobbyist for some major companies in the northwest area of the state, and he was holding a fundraiser for his clients. Also, he wasn't human—at least not completely—which made him an excellent fit for politics.

"Stop right there!" I screamed after the fiend. I watched him hightail it around the corner of the eight-foot-high hedge that surrounded the ornamental grounds. Good. The partygoers wouldn't see me take ol' Hennessey down. Bless the face-melting heat of the Missouri summer—no one inside would venture outside lest common sweat ruin their designer duds.

Unlike my attire, the lobbyist's tailored tuxedo was perfect for hauling ass. The tight red evening dress hugged my knees and made it hard to do much but waddle like a penguin. I tottered around the shrubbery and took an awkward step forward. My heel dipped sideways, and the dewed grass kissed the side of my foot. Ack! My heels! My dearly departed sister Charlotte would be appalled at the treatment of my footwear.

I saw my target just a few feet away from another turn in the boxed hedge. I had scoped out the whole area the day before, so I knew the landscape. I also knew I couldn't catch him before he entered the maze surrounding the marble inlay fountain with its ode to Hennessy himself. Yeah. There was a bronze statue of him holding an American flag in one hand and a champagne bottle in the other.

"I just want to talk," I lied. "Don't you want to make a deal?"

Offering to make a deal to a demon was the equivalent of showering a chocolate addict with truffles. He stopped about twenty feet from me and turned back, his head hitching to one side. "So," he sniffed. "You're the Madder. You don't look like much."

I smoothed my dress, and lifted my chin, and poured on my best Southern drawl. "That's just a mean thing to say, sir. Especially to a lady." My "a"s sounded like "uh"s, and I dropped the "r" in sir. I was pretty proud of the fact that I'd managed to master the non-regional American dialect over the years, but every once in a while, it was fun to pull out the Southern Belle.

The demon in the Hennessey suit snorted, the fear draining from his blue eyes. "Frankly my dear, I don't give a damn."

I loved when they underestimated me. But I hated when they quoted *Gone With the Wind*. I dropped the accent. "I'm not Scarlett, and you're for damn sure not Rhett, so let's cut the shit."

He raised a brow. "You know, now that I see you, I don't know what all the hoopla's about." Curling his lip, he sized me up. "You're kind of doughy."

"That hurts." Actually, it did. I don't care how old you are, women are women everywhere, and none of us want to be thought of as doughy—he might as well have said thick, or hippy, or FAT. Sure, I had curves—some in the wrong places—and my size D breasts were threatening to spill over the top of the borrowed dress, but it didn't give this

235

impostor the right to judge. Especially this skinny, short, pale, and balding imposter about to get his face kicked in.

The "hoop-la" as he called it was the buzz in the under-world about a rogue minion going bat-shit all over demon ass. That rogue would be me, Olivia Madder. Of course, this wasn't the first time I'd been called "the Madder." I've been tracking demons for more than a hundred years and some change. And while I'm not always successful in sending them back to Hell, I had a seventy-seven percent completion rate. Charlotte would've called that bragging, but I called it awesome.

"Tell me about the deal," said Hennessey. "It better be good."

The deal was that I was going to fry him. Now that he had me good and pissed, it was time to teach this uncouth jerk what all the fuss was about. I bent my knee up until I could reach my shoe and nearly fell over as the dress caught on the stiletto. In my struggle to stay upright, the back of the dress ripped at the seam.

Hennessey snorted again. "Had I known that stripping was part of your routine, I might not have been so quick to run."

"Right. You insulted my curves, but now you want to see them?" With the breeze literally at my backside, but infinitely more room to move, I toed off the other shoe so I could get good balance on the balls of my feet.

The demon, undoubtedly baffled, raised a brow. "I don't

turn down any opportunity to view the naked female form. Especially given the deficits of my current abode. So, please, do continue bursting out of your clothes."

I flipped him the bird with my free hand, before using my other hand to fling my beautiful red stiletto at him. He seemed startled to be the target of a Frisbee-ing shoe—so you can imagine his surprise when the spiked heel pierced his left eye. I was surprised, too.

I was aiming for his forehead.

A heel between the eyes wouldn't kill the demon, but it would paralyze him long enough for me to work the spell needed to drive him from this plane of existence.

He howled as he toppled onto the well-manicured bluegrass. After a moment, his howls quieted, and he sat up, slack jawed, and stared at me with his remaining blue eye.

"You rotten bitch." He pointed to the red shoe protruding from his face. "Do you have any idea how hard this body was to come by? And now you've gone and ruined the freaking eyeball."

"If it's any consolation, I didn't mean to hit you in the eye."

"Apology not accepted." He grabbed the heel and struggled to disengage it from his face. "I'm sending you the bill for the blood on my tuxedo."

I leveled my gaze at the demon — oh, sure, he was in human skin, but you can wrap a pile of dog shit in silk, and it's still dog shit, if you catch my meaning — grabbed my other shoe off the ground and tried to walk as menacingly toward my prey as the constricting dress would allow.

I shouldn't have bothered. Hennessey didn't even notice. In fact, he was too busy with shoe extraction to realize I was now standing right beside him.

"What in the name of Moloch is this fucking thing made of?" he yelled.

Iron dipped in holy water and blessed by a white witch, but I wasn't going to tell him that. I held up the other shoe and clicked the steel tip of the heel. A fan of barbs flicked out in a golf ball sized circle. I hit the tip again, and they retracted. The stilettos were my favorite, albeit least comfortable, weapons in my arsenal.

I grabbed the embedded shoe and told the demon, "Hold still."

He tilted his head to the right to give me better access. "Thanks."

Idiot. It was my stylish footwear protruding from his head, and somehow, he thought I was going to help remove it.

"Try not to damage the rest of the face," he ordered. "It's going to be difficult enough to heal the eyeball."

I lowered my head slightly, put on my sweetest smile, and spoke softly. "Don't you worry, honey," I said as I swung my right arm in an arc, "a mangled face is the least of your problems."

"Wait. What?" He looked up at me just in time to realize my intent. Still smiling, I buried the other heel deep into his forehead. *Thud. Crunch. Squish.*

"You suck," the demon mumbled as his left eyelid froze open and he dropped to the ground.

I knelt next to him and, in a gesture taken straight from the offended Southern Belle handbook, I slapped his bloodied face. "That's for your unkind comments about my appearance." I wiped my soiled hands on the demon's shirt. The rusty scent of blood mixed with the fragrance wafting from the colorful flowers planted along the hedges. Well, that was certainly a metaphor of my life— beautiful horror.

All that was left was to send the gored creature back to Hell — once he told me what I wanted to know.

I'd made friends with an Army interrogator back in the nineties. He told me that when they were trying to find Noriega in Panama, they would grab one of his known associates, a person low on the totem pole and easy to find, and make the guy tell them about the next associate, whom they'd go and find, and make that person tell about another one, and so on until they had the location of the tyrant narrowed down.

My focus was less goal-oriented. I only needed to know where to find my next demon. I didn't give a crap about the boss. He was easy to find but impossible to get rid of, so I had to satisfy myself by dispatching all his lackeys. I relied on a website called DemonsAreAmongUs.com. Its forum was filled with quackery from delusional maniacs who blamed demonic possession for every bad thing in their lives, you know, like their local gas station hiking up the price of super unleaded. Sometimes, though, there would be a post that rang of truth, like the awful one I'd read about the demon Lazul.

Unfortunately, this demon was not Lazul. But he was higher on the pecking order in this particular demonic territory—and he would know where to find the asswipe I really wanted to smite. In Kansas City, Lazul had possessed a young woman who'd committed suicide by overdosing on her antidepressants. She'd been declared dead, and her grieving parents were left alone with the corpse to say their goodbyes. Then the fiend had popped into the corpse, growled obscenities, and yelled, "I am Lazul!" The parents screamed as a demon inhabited their daughter's body. He escaped the hospital before anyone could figure out what was happening.

It was the mom's post, and the particular mentions of rotten-egg smell and glowing red eyes, that sent me after the asshole.

"That's just unsavory," a sweet voice said from behind me, slightly aghast.

"Indeed," another voice agreed, but with more interest than disgust.

"Eww," the final voice mewled. "There's goo leaking from his face."

I rolled my eyes and looked at the three young women now crouched over my shoulder, one brunette, and two blondes — the twins — decked out in full-on bustles and bonnets. Charlotte was more practical than our younger sisters, so her dress was made from pink cotton edged with tiny white flowers. The twins wore pale yellow and lavender chiffon frocks with matching lace gloves and bonnets. Not even death could force my sisters into anything less than their finest attire.

"Go away." I shooed at them. "I'm working."

"Now, Olivia," Char chided, crossing her arms tight against her chest. "Is that any way to greet your sisters?" The way she said sisters, sounded like *sistuhs*.

"Y'all are a distraction I don't need at this moment, Char." I turned the demon's head and held his left eyelid open with my thumb. "Eliza, you probably don't want to watch this."

My youngest sister was squeamish, but mostly because she had an empathic streak a mile wide. Even as a small child on the farm she'd bury dead mice—much to the annoyance of our barn cats that had killed the critters. I imagined that she would've been a social worker or something similar had she lived in this day and age.

I dug my index finger into the demon's unmarred eyeball.

"Olivia!" Eliza screeched, her skirts swishing as she skittered backward.

"I told you not to watch."

She buried her face in her hands. The eye gave a little squeak when I breached the surface, and fluid seeped out. It was yucky, but trust me, I've done worse. After a few seconds of digging, I located the bottom of each heel and clicked the barbs closed.

"You used to be the epitome of social standard, Olivia." Charlotte tisked.

"I used to be a lot of things," I said. I glanced at her. "We all did."

Charlotte's gaze fastened on the shoe as I pulled on it. "Careful!" she chided. "It took forever to fix those heels the last time you yanked them out of a vessel's forehead."

"I remember." Considering, I'd done all the work. "I made sure the barbs are closed this time," I told her.

Charlotte had a knack for fixing things. Even with genteel upbringing, Charlotte had always been at home among the farming equipment, fixing broken plows and taking apart tools to figure out how they worked. Poppa, a widowed father, would send us once a week into town to visit with our Aunt Elizabeth, who tried her best to turn us into delicate Belles, but when we were on the farm, Poppa allowed us the freedom of doing more than just house chores. Eliza became an expert on farm animals, pigs, cows, and the like. While Elise, spent all her time reading medical papers she could borrow from Dr. Beauregard Jenkins, a local surgeon, whom she sometimes volunteered with.

Even so, Charlotte couldn't actually get her hands on mechanical objects, but I could, so she walked me through the building and fixing of my demon-hunting weaponry.

Elise, the older of my twin sisters, crouched down for a closer look at the facial damage. I opened the small red clutch and grabbed the three-inch silver rod. I extracted the heel and replaced it with the rod in the center of the demon's forehead. I wiped ocular fluids, brain, and blood from the stilettos onto the demon's shirt, and then slipped them back on my feet.

"I think he has a melanoma on his forehead," Elise said, pointing to a mole on Hennessy's scalp. "It's rough, uneven in color and shape, and I'm sure he never wears sunscreen." She shook her head. "I saw one that looked just like it on Discovery Medicine."

If Elise had been born in modern times, I had no doubt she would be in medical school on her way to being a doctor. I could wish a thousand times my sisters to have different fates, and it wouldn't change a damned thing. Moloch had made sure of that.

I waved at my siblings. "Okay, shoo. Show's over, nothing to see here. Time to go. Last call. Vamoose. Am-scray even."

"You don't have to be rude," said Elise.

"Actually, I do." My sisters could ignore polite, but rude got their attention. Hooking my arms under the demon's armpits, I dragged him around the next hedge. "I'm busy at the moment. I don't have time for niceties. Sorry." Besides, the demon's master—and mine—would be showing up shortly, and I didn't want my sisters anywhere near the foul creature.

All three of them "hmphed" at the same time, then shimmered from sight. Every time they did that, I felt a lightning strike of guilt. The fact that my sisters were ghosts was in no small measure my fault.

I unhooked the chain from the clutch and formed a small circle on the ground next to the paralyzed body. Like the rod, it was made from silver. Demons had what I thought of as a severe allergy to pure silver. Even though I was a minion, the precious metal only felt warm on my skin. It didn't burn.

I'm not evil. Not yet.

I took matches, a votive candle, an orange spice incense cone, a vial of sea salt, a cigarette, and a tiny bell out of the purse. All the items were necessary to the "casting out the boogeyman" spell. Sure, it had another name, a much more complicated, can't hardly get around all the vowels kind of name, but my former demon-hunting partner had deemed it "casting out the boogeyman" and so, that's what we called it.

The familiar heartache threatened to derail my attention. It had been fifty-six years since I'd said goodbye to David Jensen—and yet, it still felt like yesterday. If you're wondering how long it takes to get over that kind of loss, the answer is never.

I poured salt around the silver chain, then I placed the candle and the cone of incense on the north and south edges respectively, struck a match and lit them both. Lifting the demon's hand, I put it inside the loop.

Ugh. I so didn't like this part. I pulled the rod from Hennessey's forehead. The demon howled with rage and pain, his whole body twisting and jerking, except for the trapped hand. His human face contorted in sheer agony. Like I said, silver was bad ju-ju for the damned, and the sea salt made it impossible for the Hellspawn to eject from its host.

That, along with the gaping holes where his eyes used to be, made me shudder inside, a weakness I refused to show to the monsters.

"Hush now," I said, sitting down next to him and trailing my fingers on his brow. "Or the pin goes back in."

"What do you want, Madder?" he asked through gritted teeth.

After all these years, it was still hard to watch human vessels wither under the spell. Sometimes the demons had a shade attached to them, not a ghost exactly — not like my sisters, more like residual energy repeating its traumatic cycle of death over and over. Especially in the newly possessed.

This body didn't have a shade.

It meant this fiend had taken up residence for at least a couple of decades. Hennessy's shade no longer lingered in this realm. "Tell me where I can find Lazul, and I'll let you go." *To Hell.* The Madder wasn't known for mercy to demonkind, and yet, they seem to always believe I'd let them go back to creating havoc for humans.

"I'd rather claw out *your* eyes," the demon rasped.

"Promises, promises." I tapped the hole in his forehead. "Remember who's in charge."

"Bitch!"

"Wow. I hope you don't kiss your mother with that mouth."

"My mother is Sin and Death, and she will feast on your innards while you roast in pits of eternal fire," he screamed, spittle forming in the corners of his lips.

"I know I'm from the South an' all, but I really don't like barbecue." Ugh. He was being stubborn. More stubborn than the average demon who'd roll on another demon to prevent getting a hangnail, let alone the pain of having his hand surrounded by the equivalent of burning pitch.

The body lurched, the empty orbital sockets seemingly staring at me, and Hennessey's voice took on an unnatural tone. "My master will come for you. In the bowels of Hell, you will burn forever. Tenfold, a palsy will fall upon your soul. Tenfold, you will beg for mercy that will never come. Tenfold—"

"Yeah. I got it. Tenfold." I shook my head. "I've heard it all before, asshole." He wasn't going to give me Lazul. From experience, most demons who talked did so in the first minute. This is what I got for trying to go through the slightly higher-ups in the demonic command chain. They weren't as easily broken. Damn it. I really wanted Lazul. Those traumatized parents deserved to put their daughter to rest properly. An empty coffin in the cold ground would be a shitty reminder that her demon-possessed body was running around doing Moloch knew what.

I picked up the cigarette, struck another match, and lit it. Leaning over, I blew a puff of smoke into the demon's face. Cyanide, a by-product of tobacco processing, was a necessary agent in the spell. It didn't take much, and cigarette smoke was the easiest way to transport the minuscule amount of poison, which is why you'd never catch one of Hell's agents smoking.

"Wait. What is that?" His nose twitched as the toxic wisps traveled into his nostrils.

He couldn't see what I was doing, but he realized what was about to happen. Beneath us, the ground shook as the demon fought to release himself from the body before I did. The thing about the boogeyman ritual was that when I used it to expel demons, they got a one-way ticket to Hell. No return trips. It was one of the more satisfying aspects of sending Moloch's lackeys back to the Pit. Time for the *pièce de résistance*. I rang the small bell. Its faint tinkle was reminiscent of a toddler's giggle.

The body instantly stilled.

The demon was gone.

Okay, so most people might have been expecting something spectacular, like out of *Supernatural*. All black smoke, fire, brimstone, explosions, and drama, but nope, just gone.

I'd expected fireworks the first time I cast a demon out of this plane, so I understand the disappointment.

I repacked my clutch, attached the chain before putting it over my shoulder, and got to my feet. I kicked the vessel's thigh. "Take that, Moloch."

Upon mentioning his name, the demon lord burst into existence in front of me.

Fantastic.

Not.

PARANORMAL MYSTERIES & ROMANCES

By Renee George

Witchin' Impossible Cozy Mysteries

www.witchinimpossible.com

Witchin' Impossible (Book 1)

Rogue Coven (Book 2)

Familiar Protocol (Booke 3)

Mr & Mrs. Shift (Book 4)

Barkside of the Moon Mysteries

www.barksideofthemoonmysteries.com

Pit Perfect Murder (Book 1)

Murder & The Money Pit (Book 2)

The Pit List Murders (Book 3)

Peculiar Mysteries

www.peculiarmysteries.com

You've Got Tail (Book 1) FREE Download

My Furry Valentine (Book 2)

Thank You For Not Shifting (Book 3)

My Hairy Halloween (Book 4)

In the Midnight Howl (Book 5)

My Peculiar Road Trip (Magic & Mayhem) (Book 6)

Furred Lines (Book7)

My Wolfy Wedding (Book 8)

Who Let The Wolves Out? (Book 9)

Madder Than Hell

www.madder-than-hell.com

Gone With The Minion (Book 1)

Devil On A Hot Tin Roof (Book 2)

A Street Car Named Demonic (Book 3)

ABOUT THE AUTHOR

I am a USA Today Bestselling author who writes para-normal mysteries and romances because I love all things whodunit, Otherworldly, and weird. Also, I wish my pittie, the adorable Kona Princess Warrior, and my beagle, Josie the Incontinent Princess, could talk. Or at least be more like Scooby-Doo and help me unmask villains at the haunted house up the street.

When I'm not writing about mystery-solving werecougars or the adventures of a hapless psychic living among shapeshifters, I am preyed upon by stray kittens who end up living in my house because I can't say no to those sweet, furry faces. (Someone stop telling them where I live!)

I live in Mid-Missouri with my family and I spend my non-writing time doing really cool stuff...like watching TV and cleaning up dog poop.

Follow Me On Bookbub!